CW01429172

The Coat of Arms Killer

THE
COAT OF ARMS
KILLER

FRANCES LLOYD

DI Jack Dawes Murder Mystery 12

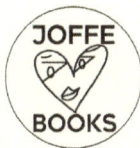

JOFFE
BOOKS

Joffe Books, London
www.joffebooks.com

First published in Great Britain in 2025

© Frances Lloyd

This book is a work of fiction. Names, characters,
businesses, organizations, places and events are either
the product of the author's imagination or are used
fictitiously. Any resemblance to actual persons, living
or dead, events or locales is entirely coincidental.
The spelling used is British English except where fidelity
to the author's rendering of accent or dialect supersedes
this. The right of Frances Lloyd to be identified as author
of this work has been asserted in accordance with the
Copyright, Designs and Patents Act 1988.

No part of this book may be used or reproduced in any
manner for the purpose of training artificial intelligence
technologies or systems. In accordance with Article
4(3) of the Digital Single Market Directive 2019/790,
Joffe Books expressly reserves this work from the text
and data mining exception.

Cover art by Dee Dee Book Covers

ISBN: 978-1-80573-005-7

Nemini Confidite
A web of intrigue, lies, deceit — and murder.

PROLOGUE

Lord Hugo Fitzwarren, 27th Baron of Richington, could trace his family in an unbroken line as far back as 1066, when it is documented that William de Warren, a powerful Norman baron, was present at the Battle of Hastings. It was a Norman custom to disallow the use of the father's surname while he was still alive, hence his son acquired the prefix Fitz — son of — Warren. When William de Warren died, his son then became William de Warren II and so on. In 1215, a group of powerful barons, including a Fitzwarren, could no longer stand King John's failed leadership and despotic rule and forced him to put his seal to 'The Articles of the Barons'. A formal document was then created by the royal chancery and this was the original Magna Carta.

Lord Hugo was immensely proud of his ancestor's involvement in bringing about 'The Law of the Land' in opposition to the King's autonomous commands. A voluble raconteur, it was Hugo's, favourite after-dinner speech, much of it outrageously embellished with tales of medieval derring-do to create the swashbuckling Errol Flynn effect. As mentioned in the Domesday Book of 1086, the Barons de Warren were granted many lordships, mainly in Yorkshire, but Lord Hugo's modest 2,000-acre country estate, Fitzwarren Farm, was in the Cotswolds, where he farmed rare breeds of cattle, goats, pigs and sheep. Under the expert guidance of estate manager, Adam Baker, his animals won many awards at county shows and became much sought after as breeding stock.

But Lord Hugo's main business was in financial services. Some areas paid significantly more than others and it was his multi-million involvement in investment banking, private equity and hedge funds that enabled him to maintain Fitzwarren Hall — a magnificent house on the Thames that had hardly changed since Henry VIII roamed the country. Gloomy portraits of bygone barons in varying degrees of decay — both the paintings and the barons — glared down from the galleried landing while an alarming collection of weaponry adorned the walls of almost every room. Lord Hugo's daily commute to his office in the city was often by a chauffeur-driven motorboat, one of a pair kept in the boathouse on the river for transport and for the use of weekend visitors.

Hugo's wife, Lady Helena was over forty but still strikingly attractive. In her day, she had been a supermodel and had graced the front pages of many fashion magazines. She and Hugo had met when he was in Switzerland on business and she was modelling big brand ski wear on the slopes. For his part, it wasn't so much a love match as whether she would be a suitable vehicle for the next Baron Fitzwarren. She fancied a title and a lifestyle that didn't involve freezing her tits off in several feet of snow, wearing a skimpy ski bunny suit and little else. Now, she filled her time with shopping, lunching with her lady friends and Pilates workouts to maintain her figure, which was well-preserved despite the ravages of time and two pregnancies.

Her son, the Honourable Rupert Fitzwarren — destined to become the 28th Baron — owned an art gallery in the city. The Fitz Gallery as it was called, had been a graduation present from his paternal grandmother, the Dowager Baroness Lady Beatrice Fitzwarren. Rupert's degree in Fine Arts had been a dismal after-thought but since he had shown no enthusiasm for either the military or the church, art had seemed his best option. He was dissolute, self-indulgent and a serial philanderer having inherited his mother's dazzling good looks and her lack of moral compass. Rupert's wife, Lady Louise, was decorative in an understated way. Before her marriage, she had worked as a nursery assistant so was content with a comfortable life and the only task expected of her — the eventual production of a 29th Baron.

Rupert's younger sister, the Honourable Charlotte was the most flamboyant member of the Fitzwarren family. Growing up, she had been excluded from three expensive public schools for disruptive behaviour. Nevertheless, 'Charlie' was very popular with her fellow students and considered a natural leader. Unfortunately, this talent had included leading her chums in unseemly pranks, such as mooning from the back of the school bus taking them to church. For this transgression, they had each received a hundred lines: *Body parts should never be revealed in a school setting.* Thus, when Charlie videoed a steamy liaison between the games mistress and the groundsman in the cricket pavilion, it had gone viral on the school's website with the now legendary caption: *Body parts should never be revealed in a school setting* and Charlie was chucked out yet again. On reaching eighteen, the Honourable Charlotte rejected an expensive finishing school in Switzerland and quickly found her niche on Fitzwarren Farm, where she exercised the horses and helped Adam Baker and his daughter tend the animals.

After the death of her husband, Lord William, in a boating accident, the Dowager Lady Beatrice had moved out of the main house into what she whimsically termed the 'granny annexe' but which was, in reality, a self-contained and very well-appointed Dower House in the grounds. At almost seventy, she was still fit and as she put it, 'still had all her marbles'. In summer, she could be seen racing one of the motorboats along the Thames with a champagne picnic in the back, to share with her gentleman friend, who owned a house down the river.

Lady Beattie's seventieth birthday was imminent and Lord Hugo had planned a grand ball for his mother to celebrate. The staff of Fitzwarren Hall plus many helpers from the village had been engaged to decorate the house and grounds and serve the food and drinks. A string quintet was booked to provide elegant background music. Friends and acquaintances from all corners of the community had been invited including senior officers from the police service, top government officials and members of the press. It was to be a glittering occasion, recorded in the annals of the Fitzwarren family and like the Magna Carta, it would be remembered for a very long time to come.

CHAPTER ONE

Detective Inspector Jack Dawes tried for the third time, to fasten his bow tie. He stood closer to the mirror but it didn't help. He'd never been any good with the ones you had to tie yourself. He always ended up with one side of the butterfly bigger than the other or the whole thing fell apart as soon as he let go.

'Come on, darling. The taxi will be here in a minute.' His wife, Corrie, bustled in to see what was taking him such an age.

'It's this blasted tie.' He pulled it apart yet again. 'Can't I wear my clip-on one?'

'Certainly not! This is a swanky birthday bash for the Dowager Baroness Beatrice, not Ladies' Night down the rugby club. You won't see anyone at Fitzwarren Hall wearing a tacky, clip-on bow tie.'

'Yes, but those blokes have a valet or a footman to do it.'

'Footperson,' corrected Corrie. 'And I don't expect they do — not these days. Most of the aristocracy have learned to dress themselves. Come here, I'll tie it for you.'

This wasn't as straightforward as it sounded given that Jack was six-foot-three and Corrie was a smidgeon under five feet.

'You'll have to sit down.'

Jack sat on the edge of the bed.

'That's no good. I can't tie it facing you. I need to reach round from behind, otherwise I get my left and right muddled up.'

'Well, climb up on the bed behind me,' suggested Jack.

She sighed. 'You may not have noticed — in fact, I'd be amazed if you had — but I'm wearing my posh frock. My ONLY posh frock. It's full-length mulberry silk and a crease magnet. What do you imagine it'll look like after I've clambered about on the bed?'

'Sorry, sweetheart.' Jack was contrite. 'You look stunning. It's just that I'm used to seeing you in your chef's whites. In fact, I'm surprised you're not catering this shindig yourself.'

'Hardly. I heard that Lord Fitzwarren has hired a team of chefs from one of the arty-farty, up-their-own-Michelin-star, tiny-portions-in-the-middle-of-a-plate restaurants in London. He wouldn't be interested in a provincial set-up like Coriander's Cuisine. And anyway, I'm looking forward to trying food I haven't had to cook myself.' She pulled out the stool from under the dressing table. 'Sit on there and I'll fix your tie.'

* * *

The taxi cruised slowly up the long winding drive to Fitzwarren Hall in a convoy of big, luxury cars. The rows of Italian cypresses either side were strewn with lights and lanterns that twinkled in the frosty night air.

'Ooh, isn't this pretty?' Corrie was impressed. 'They've gone to a lot of trouble.'

'Hmm,' replied Jack.

'You're making that noise,' accused Corrie.

'What noise?'

'The one you make when you're being negative.'

'I'm not being negative — I'm just not sure why we're here, that's all.' Jack looked out of the back window at the long tail of cars following along behind and was filled with trepidation.

'We're here,' asserted Corrie, 'because we were invited.'

'No, we weren't,' argued Jack. 'DCS Garwood and his wife were invited. We're here because they're abroad on holiday. We were brought on from the subs bench at the last minute.'

'Like I said, that's a very negative attitude,' admonished Corrie. 'Given our busy lives, we hardly ever get to dress up and go out somewhere smart so I'm going to enjoy it and so should you.'

'OK, I'll try, but I never know what to say to people in these situations. They make me nervous and I talk gibberish.' Jack was already feeling uncomfortable just thinking about it.

'I see, so you're perfectly happy questioning some poor miscreant in an interview room down the nick but not exchanging pleasantries with people that you haven't actually arrested for murder.'

'Something like that, yes.'

They finally arrived and the taxi pulled up alongside the white columns of the portico where uniformed staff were waiting to welcome guests and guide them inside. One of them stepped forward and opened the taxi door. Corrie gathered up her evening bag and wrap, and stepped out as elegantly as her small, rotund figure would allow. Jack took a deep breath, unwound his tall, wiry frame from the car and followed her.

'Don't stand too close to me when we get inside,' Corrie muttered from the corner of her mouth. 'If we stand side by side, we look like the number ten.'

* * *

The cavernous entrance hall was spectacular — wine-coloured walls with an elaborate plaster work ceiling and a black and white marble floor, laid out in an intricate design. Life-sized suits of armour stood on square pedestals and on the walls, an array of long swords, lances, metal-headed maces, battle-axes and daggers evidenced the medieval weapons without which no well-dressed Fitzwarren knight would have ventured forth onto a battle field.

This wasn't an occasion for balloons and banners proclaiming 'Happy 70th Birthday Beattie' but there were scores of extravagant floral arrangements on plinths and hundreds of illuminated garlands that emphasised the importance of the celebration. Corrie was immediately scooped up by two ladies in glamorous dresses for whom she had catered dinner parties in previous weeks. Neither was the type to sweat over a hot stove and they were anxious to discuss her availability for a charity gala evening they were arranging. Jack wandered into the main reception room and stood marvelling at the impressive decor and fidgeting with his tie, which felt like it was garrotting him. It was very crowded and a passing waitress offered him a glass of chilled champagne from her tray which he accepted gratefully. He was about to sip it when he felt a heavy hand on his shoulder and heard a booming voice in his ear.

'Evenin' Dawes. Good turnout, what?'

Jack turned to see Commander Sir Barnaby Featherstonehaugh, in a dinner suit that looked as if it had come from a retro vintage store and smelled strongly of moth balls. He made a mental note to tell Corrie that the Commander was wearing a clip-on bow tie. 'Oh . . . er . . . good evening, Commander. Nice to see you. Yes, it is a good turnout. Er . . . very good.' He stuttered, nervously.

'Where's your good lady? Carrie, isn't it?'

'It's Corrie, Commander, short for Coriander. Er . . . she's around here somewhere.' Jack looked around, hoping she would come and rescue him. She was good at this kind of thing.

'No need to call me *Commander*, Dawes. Not tonight. This is a social occasion after all, and we aren't in uniform. Plain *Sir* will do.'

'Yes, of course, sir.'

Sir Barnaby took yet another glass of champagne off the tray as it came past. He burped loudly. 'Can't abide this fizzy stuff — makes me fart.' He gulped some and burped again. 'Pity old Gee-Gee couldn't make it.' Gee-Gee was his nickname for DCS George Garwood. 'Swanning about the Mediterranean, apparently. His wife insisted she was exhausted and wouldn't give up her cruise. I told him he should have put his foot down. After all, this is an important function and senior police officers' wives are expected to accompany their husbands on such occasions.'

'Is Lady Lobelia with you, sir?' asked Jack.

'No. It's her bridge night.' He looked around at the gathering and lowered his voice. 'Rum lot, the Fitzwarrens, don't you find? I remember the old boy, Lord William. Died some years ago when his motorboat crashed. Nasty business. It caught fire. He and his chauffeur were both killed. There was an investigation but nothing came of it. Rumour was that the chauffeur had been drinking. Course, they were burnt to a crisp so they couldn't prove anything.' A man wearing a kilt, sporran and Prince Charlie jacket began waving to him from the top of a very ornate staircase. 'Good Lord, there's old Scotty Mackintosh.' Sir Barnaby waved back. 'Used to be with the Home Office. Runs a top law firm with his son now, worth a fortune.' He set off across the room to speak to him. 'Anyway, enjoy your evening, Dawes.' He gave him a cursory wave over his shoulder. 'Give Cherry my regards when you find her.'

Sometime later, Corrie still hadn't reappeared and Jack had exhausted any interest he'd had in looking at the Fitzwarrens' family history paraphernalia, and there was a great deal of it. As well as all the weaponry, suits of armour and paintings, there were coats of arms, family crests, genealogy charts and parchment scrolls documenting the Fitzwarren barons' activities right back to the Magna Carta. It seemed to Jack that this interest in family ancestry was bordering on an obsession.

The Richington Ladies String Quintet was on the tenth iteration of Boccherini's Minuet — sawing away at their instruments with grim determination. He looked at his watch, wondering when it would be acceptable to ring for the taxi. Then he spotted Corrie, coming from the direction of the kitchens. He caught up with her.

'You've been gone for ages. What have you been up to?'

'I've been watching a chef balance a morsel of cream cheese on a Ritz cracker, tweezer viola petals on top and pretend it's a canapé. If that's the kind of thing we're getting to eat, we'll call in at Corrie's Kitchen on the way home for a burger and fries.'

Corrie's Kitchen was a very successful arm of Coriander's Cuisine that provided good quality online and takeaway food at reasonable prices. It was very popular with hungry people on their way home from work and who didn't have the time or the inclination to cook. What had started with Corrie as a one-woman enterprise in a small industrial unit on the edge of Kings Richington had grown into something of a culinary empire, providing food at both ends of the gastronomic spectrum.

'I could really fancy a burger. I'm starving.' Jack drooled at the thought. 'Could we leave now, do you think? I mean, who's going to notice? I've already done my duty and tugged my forelock at the Commander.'

'No, we can't go yet. Apparently, there's going to be some kind of birthday presentation to Lady Beatrice.' Corrie pointed to where a large easel had been erected on the galleried first floor landing, so that guests down below could see. It supported a six-foot painting, concealed beneath a velvet cloth bearing the ubiquitous Fitzwarren coat of arms and the motto *Nemini Confidite*. The family began to take their places around it, in order of seniority — lords, ladies and honourables.

'I thought Lord Hugo had a son and a daughter,' said Jack.

'He does,' confirmed Corrie.

'Well, who's that chap then?' Jack indicated the person standing next to the Honourable Rupert wearing an almost identical evening suit, dress shirt and tie, only in midnight blue velvet.

'That's Charlotte Fitzwarren, Rupert's sister. She's a little . . . avant-garde. She looks rather splendid in that dinner jacket, don't you think? I love the 'mullet' haircut. It really suits her. Such beautiful burnished auburn hair. The glamorous blonde lady who looks like she belongs in a Vogue magazine is Lady Helena, their mother.'

'She doesn't look old enough,' blurted Jack, unwisely.

Corrie scowled. 'That's because she doesn't have to stand all day chopping things and cooking stuff. She has it all done for her.'

Jack was saved from further reproach by Lord Hugo, who moved to the centre of the landing holding a microphone. He tapped it and it made a whistling sound. Some techie behind the scenes adjusted his woofers and tweeters and Hugo began.

'Ladies and gentlemen — dear friends and colleagues. Thank you so much for coming this evening to help us celebrate the seventieth birthday of my dear mother.' There was a ripple of applause.

The Dowager Lady Beatrice beamed at him. She was tall and regal, looking every inch a baroness in a full-length, powder blue *Alexander McQueen* evening dress and matching bolero jacket. The legendary Fitzwarren sapphires gleamed a rich royal blue in her ears and around her throat — a symbol of love, loyalty, power and wisdom. The late Lord William Fitzwarren had presented them to her as a wedding gift, claiming they came from deep within the Himalayan mountains of Kashmir and they had been a present to his grandmother from a high-ranking Hindu prince. They evoked images of maharajas, draped in spectacular jewels and riding elephants.

Corrie berated herself for thinking how Lord Hugo, who could only have been around five-feet-seven or eight, didn't quite measure up to her idea of a baron. The poor man had mousy brown hair, a pasty complexion and a big nose.

11

Corrie decided that nobility must be more about behaviour than appearance.

Hugo continued. 'As a surprise for my dear mama, I commissioned a portrait painter to paint my late father, Lord William Fitzwarren, 26th Baron of Richington, who sadly passed away in a boating accident some fifteen years ago. Fortunately, we had several photographs of him to enable a good likeness. He can now take his rightful place amongst the portraits of his ancestors, dating back to 1066 and beyond.' He reached out a hand to Beatrice. 'Mama, happy birthday. Would you like to come forward and unveil the painting?'

Everyone waited with bated breath, ready to cheer as she took hold of the cord attached to the velvet cloth and pulled. As planned, the cover slid away revealing Lord William's portrait but instead of cheers, there were gasps of shock. Someone had taken one of the medieval daggers from the wall and plunged it into his chest. Beneath it, scrawled in red paint to look like dripping blood, was the word — KILLER.

CHAPTER TWO

It was pandemonium. Cameras flashed as eager press pho-
tographers, invited to cover the occasion, took full advantage
of the opportunity to capture what would become a front-
page exposé. This was much more newsworthy than *Tatler*
shots of a *Who's Who* of the elite, guzzling champagne and
neighing dutifully to each other about how much they were
enjoying the wonderful party. In just a few moments, someone had put a dampener on a festive atmosphere and turned
it into something macabre and menacing. Confused guests
looked at each other in disbelief. Who would do such a thing
at what was considered to be society's most important celebration of the year? Everyone knew that graffiti artists were
everywhere, daubing their 'tag' on any accessible surface, but
this had gone way beyond anything that mindless vandals
might have done. This was a message.

Lady Beatrice was particularly shocked. Fearing the
effect on her weak heart, Lord Hugo took his mother's arm
and escorted her to the family's private sitting room to lie
down. The rest of the Fitzwarrens trailed behind in bewildered disarray. Their sheltered, cosseted lives meant they
were unprepared for such unpleasantness, right here on their
doorstep, as it were. Security guards, hired to prevent any

disturbance of this kind, sprinted about speaking urgently to each other on their intercoms in an attempt to co-ordinate some kind of credible control.

An unruly crowd had formed at the entrance to the improvised cloakroom where beleaguered staff struggled to find the coats of people who were now just as anxious to leave the party as they had been to attend. Outside, cars jostled to join the queue heading back down the drive.

'Well, Dawes, what are you doing about this?' Sir Barnaby appeared at Jack's elbow. 'Apart from me, you're the only working copper here so I'm assigning you as SIO to find out who did it. Bloody disgusting behaviour at the poor old girl's birthday party!'

Jack was hesitant. 'Er . . . I'm head of the Murder Investigation Team, sir. It's a homicide squad. I think this comes under the Criminal Damage Act of 1971. There's a separate team to deal with this kind of offence.'

'Yes, but they're not here, are they? And you are! Make some inquiries, man. It's the least the police can do. We don't want accusations of two-tier policing — one service for villains and another for toffs. Catch the blighter who did this and charge him.' He strode off to find his car before he got caught up in the unseemly commotion.

Corrie appeared, ready to leave, having wormed her small but solid way to the front of the queue and claimed her wrap from the cloakroom.

'Well, that was pretty unpleasant, wasn't it? I know Lord Hugo wanted the unveiling of his late father's portrait to be the climax of the evening, but not like that. Poor Lady Beatrice. It was awful for her. Who'd do a thing like that? And what did they mean?'

'That's what Sir Barnaby wants me to find out although I haven't a clue how. I can't deploy a SOCO team to look for fingerprints and test for DNA because some idiot stabbed a painting.'

Corrie chewed her lip thoughtfully. 'It could just be a childish prank gone badly wrong, I suppose.'

'I doubt it,' said Jack. 'I strongly suspect there's a lot more to it than a prank and there's worse to come.'

Corrie looked at him. 'It's your 'copper's nose' again, isn't it?'

Jack's nose, apart from being crooked and off-centre due to his rugby-playing days, was also a harbinger of crime and had served him well in the past. This was no exception.

'When somebody goes to extraordinary lengths to make some kind of statement, it rarely ends there. I think I'll have a few words with the family — find out if there have been any other similar attacks on the peers — abusive manuscripts in the post, dead ermines on the doormat, bricks through the stained-glass windows, that kind of thing. Will you be OK to make your own way home, sweetheart? I've called for a taxi.'

'Yes, I'll be fine. I'll get you a burger from Corrie's Kitchen on the way.' She kissed him and joined the throng, shuffling their way out through the opulent hallway. She smiled to herself. Less than an hour ago, Jack was feeling self-conscious in what was essentially a social situation. Now he was back in his comfort zone, investigating a crime.

* * *

Jack showed his warrant card to the security guard standing outside the Fitzwarrens' private rooms. He was directed to a smartly dressed chap who gave his name as Beach. Jack assumed he was the butler, although he doubted the woke-rati would approve of such a pejorative job title. It was more likely to be major-domo, house manager or chief of staff. Whatever he perceived his duties to be, Beach placed himself firmly between Jack and the sitting room door.

'I'm afraid the family aren't receiving visitors at the moment.'

Jack produced his ID. 'I can't say I'm surprised, Mr Beach, in view of what happened this evening. I just wanted to have a word in case the police can assist in any way. Would that be possible do you think?'

'I'll find out for you, sir.' Beach tapped on the door. There was some subdued conversation inside, then having been given the go-ahead, he showed Jack into the sitting room. If possible, it was even more sumptuous than the reception room. Two Cavalier King Charles spaniels leaped up from the hearth rug and hurtled towards him, barking. The Honourable Charlotte called a single word to them and immediately they fell silent and returned to the rug. The Dowager Lady Beatrice had changed from her evening dress into a printed silk robe with the family crest embroidered on the lapel. She was reclining with her feet up on a cream velvet sofa, surrounded by a heap of cushions and clutching a very large glass of brandy.

The rest of the family lounged around the room in various plush chairs. Rupert had taken off his jacket and tie and Charlotte had done the same. They had both kicked off their shoes. None of them looked unduly traumatized. Their mother, Helena, was stifling a sophisticated yawn — either from boredom or a surfeit of champagne. She had released her long blonde hair from its elegant chignon and let it fall around her shoulders. Nobody invited Jack to sit down.

Lord Hugo, still in full evening dress, examined Jack's ID which Beach had presented to him on a silver tray, then he stepped forward to shake his hand. 'Detective Inspector Dawes? I wasn't aware we had called the police. We were just having a nightcap before bed.'

Jack thought he was surprisingly composed, considering what had taken place earlier. 'You didn't call us, Lord Fitzwarren, we were already here. My wife and I were invited to the celebration as was Commander Sir Barnaby. He suggested I might have a word about the unfortunate incident that occurred this evening, in case the police could be of some help.'

Hugo waved a hand, dismissively. 'Oh, I hardly think a piece of random vandalism by a mindless gate crasher warrants the attention of a detective inspector from the Met, do you?'

'That rather depends on whether it *was* random or if it was targeted, sir.' Privately, Jack thought it highly unlikely that the perpetrator had been a gate crasher. The level of security had been exemplary. Nobody got in without an invitation and there were door supervisors at every entrance and exit. This had to be an inside job. 'Do you have any idea why someone would paint the word 'killer' on your late father's portrait, sir?'

'None at all. When do delinquents and layabouts have a plausible reason for doing anything? I blame social media, inciting these individuals to do exactly what they like with no concept of responsibility and no fear of reprisal.'

'It's all about breeding,' piped up the Dowager from beneath her nest of cushions. 'There's no proper class system any more. Old families like ours are an obvious target. What can you expect?'

Jack was doubtful whether he would get any further with this line of questioning but had one last try. 'Have there been any other incidents of this nature, sir?'

Over in the inglenook seat, Charlotte opened her mouth as though about to say something, but her father silenced her with a look. 'Absolutely not, Inspector. I don't know if you're familiar with the peerage system in the UK but the rank of baron is the most populated. At the last count, there were four-hundred-and-twenty-six of us hereditary barons and lords of Parliament, and that's not including courtesy titles. I'm sure if you were to contact them, a large number would report having experienced acts of violence and vandalism, simply from envy of perceived privilege. Of course, the perpetrators don't envy the crippling inheritance taxes or the massive utility bills and the costs of maintaining an historically important property such as this for posterity.'

'That's right,' agreed Rupert, suddenly emerging from his bored apathy. 'We get them in the Fitz Gallery, don't we, Lulu?' His wife nodded. 'Oiks eating ice cream while their ghastly, snotty kids run riot and put their sticky fingers over everything. They're not interested in art, they just come in to piss us off, don't they, Lulu?'

'Yes, Rupert.' Sitting next to him on a chaise longue, his wife Louise wondered vaguely whether that's how he would describe his own offspring, assuming she ever managed to produce one. She'd got used to Grannie Beattie looking pointedly at her stomach every day. She wondered how much longer it would be before Hugo decided to put her — Rupert's poor barren wife — out to grass and find another brood mare to produce a 29th baron. She had an appointment with her gynaecologist in Harley Street the next day for some test results. Perhaps he would be able to give her some good news.

'Well, if that's all, Inspector, my mother's had a shock and needs to rest.' Lord Hugo moved towards the bell to summon Beach. 'Thank you for your concern and of course, I'll be in touch if anything else occurs.'

Jack knew when he was being dismissed. He nodded goodbye and left.

* * *

It was quiet in the sitting room for some minutes, just the sound of burning logs crackling in the elegant fireplace. The family exchanged significant glances but no words. Hugo picked up the brandy decanter and refilled his mother's glass.

Then Charlie spoke. 'Pa, shouldn't we have told him about that business at the farm?'

'Whatever for?' Hugo glared at her. 'How would that have helped anybody? For goodness sake, Charlotte, for once in your life, have a thought for the honour of the Fitzwarrens.' He patted Beatrice's hand. 'Don't worry, Mama. I'll find out who's doing these things and I'll put a stop to it.' He sounded confident and assertive but in reality, he was nothing of the sort.

The family eventually drifted off to their rooms and Mrs Beach was summoned to escort the Dowager to a bedroom she'd prepared for her on the first landing. Upset and fearful, Beatrice hadn't wanted to make the journey to the Dower

House and spend the night on her own. Hugo was the last to retire, more disturbed by what had happened that evening than he was prepared to admit. He understood exactly what the message meant. What he didn't know, and this was much more disconcerting, was who had left it and how much they knew.

* * *

Corrie was still up when Jack got home, having swapped the posh frock for her Winnie-the-Pooh onesie — a more comfortable option and you didn't have to worry about creases or spilling wine down the front. She retrieved Jack's burger and fries from the oven where they were keeping warm. 'How did it go, darling?'

Jack shook off his dinner jacket and untied his bow tie, leaving it hanging loose, Frank Sinatra-style. 'Well, it didn't, really. I asked some polite questions and Lord Hugo politely stonewalled me. I was given a lecture about the state of the peerage, crippling taxes and what it costs to maintain a Grade 1 Listed building for posterity. Then the butler was summoned and I was thrown out.'

Corrie poured him a generous glass of Merlot to wash down the burger. 'Maybe there isn't anything to find out. It could just have been someone wanting to spoil the party. There are some very discontented people out there, just bent on causing trouble and upsetting people who they believe are better off than they are, but don't deserve to be. It's class envy and spite, you see it every day on social media. Clickbait that leaves out key information to attract as much reaction and indignation as possible.'

Jack realized he was starving. He bit into his burger and chewed. 'That's true but I'd bet next month's salary that there's more to it than that.'

'Copper's nose again?' asked Corrie.

'Very definitely. We haven't heard the end of the Fitzwarren saga.' He pointed to the front of her Winnie-the-Pooh onesie. 'There's a dollop of mayo on Piglet's ear.'

She wiped it off with her napkin. 'But as long as no Fitzwarrens are murdered, it won't be your responsibility, will it?'

'No, I guess not. Let's hope it doesn't come to that.' He swallowed the last of his burger and looked hopefully towards the fridge. 'Is there any of that raspberry cheesecake left from yesterday?'

* * *

Next morning, Lady Louise arranged for the chauffeur, Carson, to drive her to the consulting rooms of the Harley Street gynaecologist. The examination rooms were carefully appointed to put patients at their ease. Tasteful decor in shades of jade and taupe encouraged ladies to lie back and relax, despite sometimes being given news that, in an ideal world, they wouldn't have to hear. Now, Louise was sitting on one side of an impressive oak desk opposite the distinguished, white-haired consultant. He had one of those faces that people described as 'lived-in' and the spectacles half-way down his nose were gold-rimmed and round. She wondered, idly, if he took on the role of Santa Claus at Christmas for the kiddies in hospital. With all that white hair and a false beard, he'd be perfect. His voice when he finally spoke was soft and sorrowful. It reminded her of Sir David Attenborough, describing the demise of an endangered species. Had she known it, it wasn't far from the truth.

'I've examined your test results, Lady Fitzwarren, and I'm very sorry to tell you that it isn't good news.'

'You mean I'm still not pregnant?' She wasn't so much sad but peeved. For heavens' sakes, how much longer would she have to continue with the tedious checks and temperature charts and the disapproving looks from the old Dowager and Hugo's snide comments about substandard breeding stock?

'No, you aren't pregnant and I'm very much afraid that in my opinion, it's unlikely you will ever conceive. I'm so sorry.'

'What?' She heard herself almost shriek. 'Why ever not?'

He hesitated, trying to find the least hurtful way to explain while giving her the plain truth. 'You have contracted a sexually transmitted disease of the kind that causes irreversible damage to your reproductive organs. The scarring is extensive.'

She caught her breath, trying to process what he had said. 'But that's impossible. You carried out all the tests that the Fitzwarren family insisted on before I married. I didn't have it then and I can assure you that I have only had relations with my husband since.' The whole process of ensuring she was suitable to bear a Fitzwarren heir had been feudal, like something potential wives had to go through in the reign of the Tudors.

The consultant paused, hoping she would come to the inevitable conclusion on her own. She didn't. He realized that he would have to spell it out for her. 'In that case, Lady Fitzwarren, the only explanation I can offer is that you have contracted the disease from Lord Rupert.'

Her first reaction was — how could she have been so stupid? Her second was outrage. She was filled with fury and contempt. For all their airs and graces, the Fitzwarrens had fouled their own pretentious nest. Not only that, they had done her irreparable harm in the process. She wanted to kill Rupert. She had known when she married him that he could never keep it in his trousers, but it had seemed like a quid pro quo arrangement for a life of privilege and babies to love. As for his pathetic, obsessive father she wanted to kill him, too, for not controlling his son's behaviour. She stood up, trembling with anger and shock. 'Thank you for being so frank. Naturally, I will undergo any treatment that you recommend.'

Outside, Carson, the chauffeur, opened the door of the Bentley and she climbed in. On the journey home she calmed down sufficiently to consider her position. When her father-in-law learned of her infertility, she knew he would take steps to replace her. It would be done discreetly, of course.

21

This was a family where divorce was still looked upon as dishonour. She also knew that feckless Rupert didn't have any strong feelings for her one way or the other. Their spasmodic, joyless coupling had been perfunctory and brief, so she couldn't rely on any support from him. Well, if Lord Hugo wanted rid of her, let him try — but she wouldn't go without a fight and she'd make sure he and his toxic family came off worse. She wondered how he would react when she told him his precious son, heir to the Fitzwarren title, had given her the clap. Although, as she recalled it, Henry VIII's poor reproductive record was attributed to a sexually transmitted disease, so Hugo would probably only see it as another indication of noble birth.

* * *

Louise travelled home, all the while fuming and plotting all manner of revenge on her pox-ridden husband and the absurd, pompous little man he called father. Unknown to her or anybody else, Lord Hugo was down in one of the five remaining priest holes in Fitzwarren Hall. Constructed during the period when Catholics were persecuted by law, this space beneath the library floor was accessed through a trap door in the fireplace of the Great Parlour. It was virtually invisible, unless you knew it was there.

Hugo had rigged up a lamp and a makeshift desk so that he had somewhere private to examine what were seriously confidential papers. When you lived in a house populated by inquisitive relatives and an inordinate number of servants, dusting and tidying everything, documents recording deeply personal information and detailing life-changing decisions had to be protected at all costs. He couldn't afford any mistakes at this stage, not until it was time to reveal what he was about to do. He took great care to ensure nobody saw him coming and going and he left everything behind in a locked briefcase on the desk in the priest hole. He didn't trust the safe in his study. Equally, he couldn't trust the security of his

London office with secretaries and Napier-Smythe having access to everything. The information in the briefcase was top secret.

While Louise was planning her own private apocalypse on the Fitzwarren family, down below the library floor, trying to process potentially mind-blowing data, Hugo was plotting a much bigger one of his own.

CHAPTER THREE

One month later

Activity had been unusually slack in the incident room of the Murder Investigation Team, which always made DI Dawes uneasy. It reminded him of the old adage about London buses — you wait ages for one, then two come along at once. It wasn't that he wanted some poor unfortunate soul to be bumped off before their time, just to give him something to do, but he needed a diversion to take his mind off the weird incident with the portrait at Fitzwarren Hall, which was still nagging away in his head. For the hundredth time, he questioned why someone would go to such lengths to make a point and then not follow it up. Even if Corrie had been right and there were oddballs out there who got a kick out of shocking people, it didn't explain why they had targeted the Fitzwarrens in such a risky way.

The place had been crammed with people. There was a good chance that someone might have caught the perpetrator in the act. Jack had taken a closer look at the portrait at the time and the red paint had still been wet, so it hadn't been done weeks in advance — it had been done on the night, which confirmed his earlier suspicions of an inside job. A disgruntled member of staff with a chip on one shoulder and an axe to grind on the other, perhaps? Or one of the guests? There were plenty to choose from and they must all have had some connection to the Fitzwarrens, however tenuous, or they wouldn't have been invited. When the phone rang, it was a welcome interruption to his thoughts that were buzzing around his brain like angry bees in a hive.

DI Dawes' second-in-command, Detective Sergeant Mike 'Bugsy' Malone answered it. It was the uniformed desk sergeant. Bugsy greeted him as he always did. 'Hello, Norman, my old woodentop. What can we do for you?'

Sergeant Norman Parsloe had manned the public desk for longer than any of the present incumbents could remember and had been a consummate thief-taker in his day. His local knowledge of Kings Richington's crime and the criminals who committed it was a vital contribution to the division's clear-up rate. He came straight to the point.

'I've got a young lady on the desk who wants to report that her father has gone missing.'

'OK, well take her statement and pass it to the MISPER team.' Bugsy wondered why Norman had contacted the MIT. They only dealt with missing persons after their bodies had been found and only then if there were suspicious circumstances.

'Well, that was my first thought and obviously I would have, Bugsy,' Norman countered, 'but she specifically asked for DI Dawes to handle it. I tried to tell her that Jack doesn't deal with missing persons' cases but she says he knows the family and he'd told them to report anything unusual.'

'What's her name?' Bugsy prepared to write it down.

'She's the Honourable Charlotte Fitzwarren. Her father is Lord Hugo Fitzwarren.'

'Hang on, Norman . . .' Bugsy shouted across to Jack, 'Guv, do you know a lord called Hugo Fitzwarren?'

Jack was immediately alert. 'Yes, why?'

'His daughter's downstairs on the desk. Says he's gone missing. I reckon the old bloke has probably just wandered off looking for the pub. I mean, elderly folk escape from their nursing homes all the time, don't they? There's rarely any suspicion of murder — somebody just rounds them up, takes them back, makes them cocoa and plonks them in front of Tipping Point. I told Norman to report it to MISPER, but she says . . .'

Jack jumped up from his chair. 'Ask Norman to put her in an interview room and I'll come down. I've got a funny feeling about this one. For a start, he isn't an old bloke, only in his forties. Bugsy, you'd better come with me. I'll fill you in on the way down.'

By the time they had exited the lift next to the interview room, Jack had related the portrait incident to Bugsy, who recalled seeing a front-page article about it in the *Richington Echo.* The editor had been one of the guests and had reported it simply as 'a tasteless prank by an unknown perpetrator which had put a premature end to the evening's festivities'. Some of the nationals hadn't been quite so accommodating and had hinted at family feuds, the settling of old scores and mutinous servants.

Usually, the interview room smelled of stale sweat, disinfectant and drunk-and-disorderly old lags looking for a meal and a bed for the night. On this occasion, Jack detected a whiff of floral perfume. The Honourable Charlotte Fitzwarren was sitting at the table sipping a cup of Sergent Parsloe's tea — strong enough to float a mouse. She wore ripped jeans, a hoodie and a back to front baseball cap over her thick auburn hair.

'Er . . . Lady Charlotte . . .' Jack began, unsure of her correct title but trying not to sound too pompous.

She brushed that away. 'Please, just call me Charlie.'

The two coppers sat down in the chairs opposite. 'This is my colleague, Detective Sergeant Malone. How can we help?' asked Jack.

She came straight to the point with no preamble. 'Pa has gone missing — that is, my father, Lord Hugo Fitzwarren. You met him at Grannie's birthday party.'

'Yes, I remember.' Jack recalled Lord Hugo dismissing him with little more than an imperious wave. 'How long has your father been gone?'

'Just over a week. I wanted to report it before, but Rupert, that's my brother, said Pa wouldn't want a fuss and he'd come home when he was ready. My mother said the same. But I'm worried, Inspector. The Bentley is still parked in the garage and neither of the motorboats has gone, so what is he using for transport?'

'Might he have taken a taxi somewhere?' asked pragmatic Bugsy.

'I suppose so, but why? And why wouldn't he have told anybody? Our chauffeur, Carson, hadn't been made aware that Pa was planning a trip and Dickie didn't know either — that's Dickie Napier-Smythe, Pa's business partner.'

'What about your mother, Lady Helena?' asked Jack.

Charlie shrugged. 'I don't think Mother even noticed he was gone until yesterday when I mentioned it and even then she didn't seem bothered. Grannie's the only one of the family who's worried, like me. She's been on edge ever since that awful thing happened to Grandfather's portrait at her birthday party. I told her I was coming to see you and she said she'd be so grateful if you could help us to find Pa.'

'Has he done anything like this before?' asked Bugsy. In his experience, the MISPERS who wanted to 'get away from it all to *find themselves*' frequently made a habit of it, until someone got fed up with their antics and gave their head a wobble.

'No. Never.' Charlie was emphatic. 'And before you ask, he wouldn't have run away because he'd done something criminal. Pa would never bring dishonour to the Fitzwarren name.'

'We'll need a photograph of your father, miss.' Even though Lord Hugo was a public figure in the city where his business was located, Bugsy thought a photo might jog a few memories for those ordinary folk who were not in the habit of rubbing shoulders with the nobility.

'I thought you might, Sergeant, so I brought one with me.' Charlie opened her backpack and pulled out a picture of her father in his baron's robes, complete with ermine tails, two miniver bars and a coronet with three pearls, indicating his rank.

Bugsy was tempted to ask if she had one where he wasn't in fancy dress but thought better of it. While he wasn't a fan of pomp and pageantry, he liked to think he wasn't unnecessarily rude, either.

'Do you have CCTV at Fitzwarren Hall?' asked Jack.

'Yes, there are cameras all around the house. We've had burglars in the past so Pa had them installed at the suggestion of your commander — I think he's called Sir Barney or Barnard, something like that. They're members of the same club.'

'Well, CCTV's a good place to start.' Jack stood up. 'Leave it with us, Charlie, and we'll make some enquiries. Try not to worry. I'm sure there'll be a perfectly logical explanation and your father will turn up safe and well.' But even as he said it, Jack didn't believe it. If his gut feeling and his prognostic nose were anything to go by, this was just the next episode in a series of incidents that weren't going to end well.

* * *

Later that week, Bugsy called the whole team into the incident room for a briefing. Jack stood in front of the whiteboard where he had pinned the photograph of Lord Hugo in all his regalia.

'Now, listen up, everyone. Before you ask why a Murder Investigation Team is dealing with a missing person case, I should tell you that the Commander telephoned me earlier with a request that we launch an urgent enquiry into the disappearance of Lord Hugo Fitzwarren, who was last seen nearly two weeks ago.'

The actual conversation had been rather more direct. 'Dawes, pull your finger out, man! I should have thought you'd have found Fitzwarren by now with all the resources I've put at your disposal. How hard can it be? He isn't ill or witless — well, no more than any other member of the nobility. His MP has been leaning on me, asking what steps we're taking. I said 'bloody big ones' so it'd better be true. Keep me updated.' The call had been terminated without further pleasantries.

'I'm told that DCS Garwood will be back at work next Monday,' announced Jack. 'He's taking a few days off to recover from his Mediterranean cruise. Apparently, he suffered a few gastrointestinal problems while on board. Anyway, it would be good if we could find Lord Hugo before then or at least know for certain where he is.'

'What if he doesn't want to be found, sir?' asked DC Aled Williams. 'There are times when men of a certain age just want some peace and quiet, away from women of a certain age.'

'Or what if,' countered DC Gemma Fox, 'he's pushed off somewhere with a young mistress to evade his responsibilities and to convince himself that his manhood is still intact. It's what men of a certain age do. Either that or they buy a totally inappropriate Harley-Davidson and wobble about the streets, terrorising the neighbourhood, just to prove to themselves they aren't having a mid-life crisis.'

'Do we know if he had a young mistress or a motorbike, sir?' asked DC 'Chippy' Chippendale who always took everything literally.

'I'd be very surprised if he had a mistress, having seen his wife,' muttered Jack. He wondered if anything online would help. 'Clive, where are we with digital searches?'

Clive was the team's 'delver' into background checks, and a very good one. His job title was 'head of digital forensics' and there were few databanks that he couldn't hack into when necessary — either overtly or surreptitiously. He came forward to write on the board which served to remind everybody what they knew and what still needed to be determined.

'There has been no activity on His Lordship's phone or his bank cards since he went missing. GPS places his phone somewhere inside Fitzwarren Hall. I've had my team looking at hours of CCTV and we have a clear sighting of him being driven home in the Bentley the night he disappeared. But unless he tunnelled his way out, there were no sightings of him leaving again after that. No activity with his car apart from his chauffeur polishing it, and his motorboats haven't moved. Other members of the household have been observed coming and going quite frequently, so there's nothing wrong with the cameras.'

'I suppose one of them might have smuggled him out in the back of their car under a blanket or something,' said Aled, 'but why would they?'

'And how has he managed without using his phone or bank cards? DC Dinkley was the forensic psychologist of the team and knew how dependent people were on their support systems, both physically and emotionally.

'So what's the logical assumption?' asked Jack.

'He's still in there!' The conclusion was unanimous.

'Right,' agreed Jack. 'So what's our next move?'

'We get a search team of Sergeant Parsloe's uniforms to turn the place over,' suggested Chippy.

'That could take a while, son,' observed Bugsy. 'That house is enormous, never mind the grounds and there'll be priest holes, secret passages, dungeons — we could look for days and still not find where he's hiding. Added to which, Lord Hugo will be familiar with the layout and we aren't. If he wants to avoid being found, he could just move around the place, one step ahead of our lads.'

'And there are two other reasons why a search might not be a good idea,' added Jack. 'The cost of the resources involved would give DCS Garwood worse intestinal problems than he's already experiencing and I doubt whether the Fitzwarren family, particularly his wife and son, would agree to it.'

'Couldn't we get a warrant?' asked Chippy.

'It's unlikely,' said Jack. 'In order to get a warrant to search someone's premises, we have to satisfy a magistrate that we have reasonable grounds to suspect a criminal offence has been committed and that the premises in question may contain evidence important to any subsequent trial. 'At the moment, we don't know that any offence has been committed, do we?' Even as he said it, Jack's prophetic proboscis was sending him all kinds of assurances that an offence *had* been committed, but he doubted that a twitchy nose would be enough to convince a magistrate.

'Might he have gone to Fitzwarren Farm somehow?' asked Aled.

'Nope,' said Clive. 'We checked the cameras there, too. Plenty of pictures of Lady Charlotte coming and going in her red Mazda MX-5 but other than the estate staff, animal food delivery trucks, that kind of thing, no other traffic.'

'Suggestions anyone?' asked Jack.

'Why don't we have a word with the rest of the family, guv?' asked Bugsy. 'Somebody must know something.'

* * *

Corrie Dawes and George Garwood's wife, Cynthia, were old friends having gone to the same school and got into the same scrapes for which Corrie usually got the blame. What Cynthia lacked in academic achievement, she made up for with cunning and imagination. That afternoon, they were sitting at a window table in Chez Carlene, having lunch. The bistro, with its glazed brick facade of soothing sea-green and sky-blue, was situated in the trendy food and drink quarter of Kings Richington. It was the Michelin-starred creation of Carlene, Corrie's much-loved protégée and surrogate daughter.

Cynthia dipped a piece of baguette in her bouillabaisse. 'Honestly, Corrie, to hear George moaning and groaning, you'd think I'd booked us onto the Titanic.'

'Jack did mention that George was taking a few days sick leave after your cruise.' Corrie had opted for the moules marinière because Antoine, Carlene's partner, was an accomplished French chef and cooked them to perfection with cream, garlic and parsley. His parents, from whom he had learned his skills, owned a chain of upmarket restaurants in Paris called *Le Canard Bleu* and many of the dishes on the bistro menu had originated from there.

Cynthia savoured her Sauvignon Blanc, congratulating herself on how well it went with bouillabaisse. 'George was complaining of a gippy tummy before we even boarded. I put it down to nerves. Then when the Med got a bit choppy, he went a kind of green colour and wouldn't eat anything. He always insists on taking a suitcase full of pills and potions whenever we go away anywhere 'just in case he picks something up'. So when he went down with a stomach bug, he started dosing himself with all kinds of jollop.'

'Oh dear, poor George.' Corrie stifled a giggle.

'Eventually, everyone on board started having attacks of vomiting and diarrhoea and George declared he had contracted dysentery and took to his bunk for the rest of the cruise. I wish to point out that I was perfectly fine.'

'Will you get some kind of compensation, do you think?'

'I very much doubt it,' said Cynthia. 'The company said that following reports of passengers with gastrointestinal symptoms, they had put enhanced sanitation protocols in place, whatever that means.'

'An extra squirt of Harpic down the bogs, I expect.'

'Anyway, George said he couldn't possibly go back to work while he still had the squits, so he's sitting around at home feeling sorry for himself, in between frequent dashes to the loo. He never takes off his running shoes.'

'What a shame if all he saw on a Mediterranean cruise was the inside of the bathroom and couldn't enjoy all the free food.'

'I think I must have eaten his share. I've put on pounds. I shall have to go on a diet.' Cynthia looked at the dessert menu. 'Oh good. Carlene has crème brulée. I think I'll have that with a macaron chaser. Anyway, enough about our cruise — has anything exciting happened while I've been away?'

'Depends what you mean by exciting. We went to Lady Beatrice's seventieth birthday party instead of you and George and it was really rather horrid. Somebody put a dagger through her late husband's portrait and wrote 'killer' on it in red paint.'

'I read a bit about it in the Echo. The editor described it as a tasteless prank.'

Corrie shook her head. 'I don't believe it was and neither does Jack. It was a message of some sort for someone — goodness knows who. Now, Lord Hugo has gone missing. Nobody has seen or heard from him for almost a fortnight.'

'Aah,' said Cynthia, knowingly.

'What's that supposed to mean?' Corrie knew that her friend Cyn was a member of many posh ladies' clubs, not least her Ladies Luncheon Club. She always had her ear to the ground and could be relied upon to relay snippets of gossip that were not yet in the public domain.

Cynthia leaned close to Corrie and spoke into her ear. 'It wouldn't surprise me if Hugo going missing had something to do with Helena's latest fling.'

'Fling?' Corrie was shocked. 'You mean Lady Helena is having extra-marital . . . thingy?' She frequently wondered how women found the time or the energy, never mind the inclination.

'My dear, she's had more extra-marital . . . thingy than you've cooked hot dinners.' She tittered at her adroit change of phrase.

'Do we know who her current lover is?' Corrie couldn't help being curious and the information might be useful to Jack.

'Not for certain,' muttered Cynthia, 'but the smart money is on Dickie Napier-Smythe, Hugo's business partner. Lady Helena spends a lot of time on his cabin cruiser in the St Katharine Docks marina and I doubt if they discuss hedge funds and annuities.'

'Why hasn't Lord Hugo done something about it?' asked Corrie.

'Because if it became public, it would damage the honour of the Fitzwarrens. After all, Helena's the mother of his son, the next Baron of Richington.'

Corrie scoffed. 'That's all a bit 'Macbeth', isn't it?'

'Not to him, it isn't. Hugo takes his heritage very seriously.'

'Yes, but all the same, you'd think he'd object to serial adultery.'

'Apparently, not. Helena says he'd never divorce her, no matter what she did, although I think that might be a bit optimistic.' Cynthia picked up her spoon and gave the sugar crust on her crème brulée a whack. 'You have to wonder where he's gone, though.'

CHAPTER FOUR

Bugsy's suggestion to question the rest of the Fitzwarren family fell at the first hurdle. Helena, Rupert, Louise and eventually even Beatrice, flatly refused to cooperate. Speaking through the Fitzwarren family solicitor, James Mackintosh of Messrs Mackintosh & Mackintosh, they said they could see no good reason for police intervention and that Lord Hugo wasn't missing, he'd simply neglected to tell anyone that he was going away for a few days because his mind was concentrated on business. The solicitor went so far as to suggest that the police would be better employed dealing with the ever-increasing amount of anti-social behaviour on the streets of Kings Richington rather than wasting taxpayers' money on unnecessary and unwanted intrusion into matters that did not concern them. It prompted another brief but unambiguous telephone call from Sir Barnaby.

'Dawes, call off the search for Lord Fitzwarren.'

Jack stayed calm. 'Good morning, Commander. Has His Lordship returned home?'

'No, he hasn't, but old Scotty's son — I mean, Angus Mackintosh's son, Jamie, is the family's lawyer and apparently he and Fitzwarren had been discussing a number of important issues before he went away.'

'May I ask what those issues were, sir?'

'No, you may not. But it seems it resulted in Lord Hugo instructing his lawyers to draw up certain papers. As Mackintosh pointed out, he was not at liberty to share such information with the police without a warrant and confirmed that all would be revealed on His Lordship's return, although he had no idea when that might be. So just leave it, Dawes. This is no longer a police matter.' The call ended abruptly with Jack far from convinced.

* * *

The cosy living room in the Dower House smelled agreeably of a cedar log fire and freshly baked scones. Beatrice, elegant in a lavender cashmere sweater and navy trousers, poured proper tea from a Wedgwood teapot for herself and her companion. Sir Leonard Montgomery, looking smart as always in an open-necked shirt, slacks and blazer, had been an eminent heart surgeon in his day whose expertise had saved many lives and earned him a knighthood. Now retired, he had known William and Beatrice Fitzwarren for most of their lives and after William's untimely death, he was proud to be the Dowager Baroness Lady Beatrice's faithful gentleman friend. They visited each other regularly and sometimes went to a concert or the theatre together. He'd been present at the party when she had received a nasty shock on what should have been a joyful occasion and was now supporting her while she went through all manner of anxieties concerning the whereabouts of her son.

'You're looking pale and very thin, Bea. I hope you're taking proper care of yourself. You know your heart isn't strong.'

She frowned. 'Don't fuss, Monty. I'm fine.'

'Did Hugo say anything to you before he left?' he asked gently.

'No.'

'Surely he spoke to Helena. He must have mentioned something to his wife about going away.'

Beatrice became agitated. 'Monty, stop interrogating me. You don't understand. The dynamics of the Fitzwarren family are complicated. They don't behave like . . .'

'You were going to say . . . like normal people. Well, that's certainly true. What about the police? They're usually very good at organizing a search, especially if the missing person's in some kind of danger.'

Her eyes widened with alarm. 'Do you think Hugo's in danger, then?' Monty was putting her worst suspicions into words.

'I've no idea. It's just that if someone hasn't been seen for a while, the people close to them tend to wonder where they've gone and if they're OK. Have the police spoken to the rest of the family?'

'Only Charlotte. The others refused. They said it was an invasion of their privacy and for no good reason. They got Jamie Mackintosh to warn the police off.'

'Well, I suppose if no crime has been committed, there isn't much more the police can do. What did Charlotte tell them?'

'That she was worried, like me. Monty, if you don't mind, I think I need to go and lie down for a while.'

He stood up. 'Of course, my dear. You have a rest and I'll ring you later.'

Driving home, Sir Leonard tried to dispel suspicions that Beatrice wasn't telling him everything. He'd known about the ambiguous nature of the accident that killed Lord William but he felt that there was something more than that — something so grave that she couldn't bring herself to speak about it, not even to him.

* * *

Helena Fitzwarren sprawled elegantly on the couch, watching the moonlight glinting off the water through the portlight of Dickie Napier-Smythe's cabin cruiser. Her white cashmere sweater showed off her winter tan perfectly — the result of a

37

month's skiing in Verbier. She prided herself that her figure was as firm and shapely as it had been in her modelling days twenty years ago and she intended to keep it that way for as long as she could. She heard the welcome pop of a champagne cork from the galley as Dickie prepared her favourite cocktail. The calm, cold surface of the Thames with its oily rainbow slick slapped lazily against the side of the boat and she closed her eyes, enjoying the feeling of freedom. Whatever the consequences, she decided she had made the right decision but she needed to proceed with caution, at least for the time being. Her future was by no means secure. It would depend on what happened when they found Hugo — if they found Hugo. She was pretty sure that the rather handsome but dogged Inspector Dawes would carry on looking, whatever orders he was given to the contrary. Police detectives, she decided, were a breed apart. Poking their noses into other people's business must be in their DNA and it made them a bloody nuisance. If necessary, she'd get Jamie Mack to warn Dawes, yet again, to back off.

'Here you are, my darling.' Dickie appeared carrying a classic peach Bellini. He handed it to her. 'Sparkling, cool and classy, like you.'

She smiled, thinking how Dickie was the epitome of a successful gentleman — handsome, always immaculately dressed and with impeccable manners. The ideal companion for any occasion. Was she attracted to him? Certainly. Did she trust him? Certainly not. But for the time being, she needed to ensure she had covered all contingencies if things didn't go the way she'd planned and Dickie was her insurance. Hugo, on the other hand, her dim, ancestry-obsessed husband, thought he was so special, coming from an unbroken line of Fitzwarren barons but in fact, he was nothing special at all.

She sipped her cocktail. 'Are we staying on board tonight?'

'I'm afraid not, my angel. I'll drive you home, then I have business to attend to at the office.'

'But it's late,' she protested. 'There won't be anybody there.'

He bent to kiss her. 'That's why I need to go tonight.'

* * *

The atmosphere in the Purple Parrot nightclub was hot and so were the girls — just as Rupert liked it. Confident, laid back and a little drunk, he leaned against the bar, lining up the shots and checking out the totty. He never had to pursue women, they always came to him — like moths to a flame and with the same, damaging outcome. At university, his flat mates had called his room *The Bordello* because of the constant stream of young ladies who came and went. And they were always gorgeous, like the stunning blonde who was sashaying towards him now. No need for conversation, everything that needed to be said was done with a look, then they were off on the floor, dancing tightly against each other. Soon he was licking the sweetness from her lips and whispering his plans for the rest of the night which didn't include going home to Fitzwarren Hall.

Later, lying sated in her bed, he smoked a joint and wondered, fleetingly, if they had found his father yet. He didn't have any concerns about his mother being left on her own — she was quite capable of fending for herself, one way and another. He couldn't understand the concept of marriage in the first place. Why confine yourself to one woman, when you can have a different one every week? In the case of Louise, his father had insisted on marriage in order to carry on the legitimate line of Fitzwarren. His allowance depended on it. But once a baby happened, he'd be free to do what he liked, whenever he liked, with no threat to his financial security. He couldn't understand why Lulu hadn't knocked out a sprog already. He'd fulfilled his part of the bargain. Could there be something wrong with her insides?

* * *

Mr and Mrs Beach — Bob and Jessie — ran Fitzwarren Hall with almost military precision and had done so since Lord William Fitzwarren had been in charge. As chief of staff, Bob answered the phone, opened the door to guests, assisted in the planning of events and dinner parties and managed the wine cellar. He also had the responsibility for hiring and firing so he was directly in charge of the chauffeur and the gardeners. Jessie ensured the house was kept organized, clean and tidy while dealing with tradespeople and managing the cook and other daily staff. Together, they were the perfect combination. Very little in the household was ever neglected or overlooked. They were what is commonly described as 'treasures'.

Jessie had been dusting the artefacts in the Great Hall, when she noticed something odd. She was pretty certain it hadn't been like that the last time she was in there, but who could have moved it? She went to find Bob who was in one of the greenhouses, chatting to Ted Greenslade, the head gardener, about winter vegetables for the table. He came out to meet her when she beckoned to him.

'Bob, have you dismantled one of the suits of armour? It's the heavy jousting one on a pedestal in the south corner.'

'No, love. Why would I?'

'I thought perhaps you were having it cleaned or something. Only the helmet's missing. It looks really weird, standing there without a head. It's as if a knight has decapitated his opponent with a double-handed swipe of his broadsword.'

Bob grinned. 'You're getting very fanciful, love. It comes of living amongst all these medieval relics. But I don't think they all come alive like *Night at the Museum* and start jousting. I'll come and have a look.'

Ten minutes later, they were both in the Great Hall, looking at the headless suit of armour.

'Well, I'm blowed.' Bob scratched his head. 'Where the heck has that gone?'

'D'you think someone has pinched it?' asked Jessie.

'I doubt it. I think we'd have noticed someone leaving with a bloomin' great helmet tucked under their arm.

Besides, it's bloody heavy.' He frowned. 'I'll have to report it to Lord Hugo when he returns and he isn't going to like it. He reckons that particular suit of armour was the original worn by a Fitzwarren at the Battle of Northam in 1069.'

'And was it?'

'I shouldn't think so. It's got *Made in Sheffield 1955* stamped on the inside. It's strange because I've noticed that a lot of the so-called genuine Fitzwarren artefacts in this house are nothing of the sort. They're items that could have been picked up from any specialist collector, antique shops or even online.'

'All the same, Bob, we need to keep a lookout for the helmet in case one of the cleaners took it off, left it somewhere, then forgot about it.'

Bob patted her shoulder. 'Don't worry, love. These things have a habit of turning up where you least expect them.'

* * *

Sunday morning dawned crisp and clear. Beatrice woke with the same feeling of dread in the pit of her stomach that she'd had every morning since Hugo had disappeared. It was almost a month now and she was sure something bad had happened to her son — call it a mother's intuition. He'd been a very mindful little boy, proud of his birthright and determined to preserve it. For that reason, she'd never sent him away to school, preferring him to be educated locally where he could feel superior to the other boys. It was unlikely to have been the case had she sent him to Eton or Harrow. He'd always been closer to Beatrice than to his father, who'd bullied him because he was small and mild-mannered. Hugo had still been a relatively young man when Lord William died in the accident. He hadn't seemed to Beatrice to be overwhelmed with grief but had instantly taken over responsibility for the Fitzwarren dynasty and everything that went with it. Now, she felt an overwhelming guilt that if she had protected him better, he wouldn't have gone missing.

The rest of the family, however, seemed blithely unconcerned. Even Charlotte had been forced to accept that her father must have needed respite from the affairs of *Fitzwarren & Napier-Smythe Asset Management* and the financial burden of Fitzwarren Hall. He'd probably just gone off somewhere to recharge his batteries. What other reason could there be? After all, she did much the same thing herself when life at the Hall became too suffocating. She escaped to the honey-coloured stone farmhouse of Fitzwarren Farm in the soothing Cotswold countryside and spent time with the animals. It was her happy place. Maybe her father had one, too.

Beatrice had her breakfast in bed, boiled eggs and toast as usual, then showered and dressed. She liked frosty mornings on the river and decided it would lift her spirits if she took the motorboat down to Monty's house for coffee. He was such a loyal friend. He'd asked her to marry him virtually every day since William died, fifteen years ago. At first, it had seemed like indecent haste then as the years passed, it just seemed indecent even to contemplate such a thing. She dressed warmly in trousers, sweater and a sheepskin jacket then went down to Beach's key cabinet to pick up the keys to the boathouse.

'Are you going out alone, my lady?' Mrs Beach called to her from the kitchen. 'Do you want me to call Carson to drive you?'

'No thank you, Jessie, I'll be fine.' Fiercely independent, Beatrice preferred to manage on her own for as long as she was able.

'You will be careful, won't you, my lady?' Jessie couldn't help wondering what the family — and the staff, come to that — would do if the Dowager went missing as well as Lord Hugo. She couldn't see any of the rest of the family stepping up, apart from Miss Charlotte, but she was happy plodding about in the mud looking after her animals. Rupert was a waste of space when it came to anything requiring effort or initiative and his mother, Helena, spent her time either shopping, having her nails done or out somewhere with her fancy man. As for poor Miss Louise, Jessie felt sorry for her. Despite being married to the next in line, she seemed very unhappy and overlooked and she was a long way from her parents in Scotland. Louise often came down to the kitchen for a cup of tea and a chat.

Jessie called after Beatrice. 'Ring me on your mobile phone if you should need any help, my lady, and Carson will come and fetch you.'

Carson had been busy in Lord Hugo's absence keeping the Bentley and the other family cars in good working order so neither he nor anybody else had been out in the motor-boats. Beatrice unlocked the boathouse doors then picked her way carefully along the walkway. It was precarious and slippery where the water lapped over it and hazardous, even for a young person, so she held tightly to the guard rail until she reached the nearest boat. Climbing into it was tricky as it tended to lurch about on the water so she gripped the tiller to steady herself. She sat for a moment, relieved to be secure. But as the boat swayed beneath her, she became aware of something catching on the underside as the hull bobbed up and down. It made a metallic, grating noise that she could feel, as much as hear. She rocked the boat gently from side to side a few times. There it was again. She wondered if there was something wrong and whether she should phone Jessie to fetch Carson. Then, while she was making up her mind, the noise was explained when a waterlogged object came loose from where it had been trapped beneath the boat. It erupted to the surface with a swoosh, making first waves then bubbles.

At first, Beatrice thought it was a bundle of old clothes that someone had dumped in the river, weighted down with something metal, and it had somehow drifted into the boat-house and got snagged up. But gradually, as it emerged, it began to take the shape of a bloated body, arms and legs floating out to the side but with the head hanging forwards under the water. As she leaned out to get a better look, she could see why. The corpse was wearing the helmet from a suit of armour. Beatrice gulped, trying not to be sick. She reached in her pocket and pulled out her phone but before she could summon help, the putrefying left arm drifted closer and she could see a gold Rolex watch around the wrist. It was the one she had given Hugo on his fortieth birthday. She threw up then, deep retching paroxysms, vomiting her breakfast into her lap. She gasped, trying to catch her breath when she felt a sharp, stabbing pain in her chest that travelled down her left arm and up along her jaw. She had just time to press Jessie Beach's speed dial number on her phone and croak 'help', before she lost consciousness and slumped over the tiller.

* * *

Jessie ran to find Bob. He was polishing the brass in the dining room. 'Bob, quick, the old lady's in trouble. She called me but when I answered, she didn't speak. I could hear a kind of gasp. She needs help.'

Bob dropped the cloth. 'Where is she?'

'She said she was taking out one of the motorboats. I didn't hear the engine start up so I'm guessing she's still in the boathouse. I warned her not to go down there on her own but she's that stubborn.'

They set off at a sprint. Inside the boathouse, Bob took one look at Beatrice, dragged her from the boat onto the walkway and began chest compressions. Although trained in CPR, he made a mental note that with the Dowager's heart condition, they really should keep a defibrillator at the Hall. He spoke urgently to his wife in between rescue breaths. 'Jess, call an ambulance.'

She grabbed Beatrice's phone from the boat. 'Emergency? I'm calling from Fitzwarren Hall. Lady Beatrice is having a cardiac arrest. Yes, I'm sure. Please come quickly!'

After several minutes, Bob looked up to see Jessie staring into the water, speechless. 'Jess, what is it? What are you looking at?'

She pointed at the decomposing corpse, sodden and swollen in the water. 'It's him — it's Lord Hugo. I recognize that watch. And he's wearing the missing helmet. You said it would turn up and it has.' She pulled out the phone again. 'Emergency? I need the police, please. It's urgent.'

CHAPTER FIVE

Corrie had invited Bugsy and his wife, Iris, over for a relaxed Sunday lunch. She wanted to try out a new recipe for roast rib of beef with beef dripping chips and stilton hollandaise. If it passed the in-house test, she planned to put it on the Coriander's Cuisine menu. She knew Jack and Bugsy would simply wolf it down and reply 'fine' when she asked how it was, but she'd get an honest and more comprehensive review from Iris.

Bugsy and Iris had married late in life. Iris had been a widow for some years and Bugsy was a confirmed bachelor, or so he thought. They were perfect together and basked in each other's happiness. As part of the deal, Bugsy had acquired two step-grandchildren whom he adored. It was a joy that he had thought he would always be denied. Just being in this couple's company always lifted Corrie's spirits.

It was rare for everyone to have time off together as they were all busy people. Jack and Bugsy were up to their eyeballs in the missing Fitzwarren case. Corrie, herself, was planning a banquet menu for a charity gala and Iris worked on reception in the medical centre where her son was a doctor. This luncheon was a rare treat.

'Corrie, this is inspirational.' Iris helped herself to more hollandaise. 'The beef melts in your mouth and the stilton complements it just beautifully. You're such a clever chef.'

Corrie was delighted. 'Well, it's nice to sit and enjoy a meal in peace without Jack having to rush out . . .' She was stopped mid-sentence by Jack's mobile ringing and she made a mental note not to tempt fate in the future.

He was apologetic. 'Sorry, everyone, I'd better get that.' He went out to the kitchen to answer it and when he returned a few minutes later, he was even more apologetic. 'Bugsy, that was Norman Parsloe. They've found a body in the boathouse of Fitzwarren Hall and it looks like murder. Uniform are containing the scene and Doc Hardacre and her SOCOs are on their way.'

Bugsy stood up. 'I'll get my coat.' He kissed the top of Iris's head as he passed her chair. 'Sorry, love. That's what you get for marrying a copper.'

Corrie had seen the grim look on Jack's face. 'It's him, isn't it?'

'Yep.' Jack nodded.

'Your nose was right about Fitzwarren all along. You said there was more to come. By the way, if your nose gets any clues about the lottery numbers, you will let me know, won't you?'

He grinned. 'Unfortunately, it only sniffs out suspicious activity.' He looked longingly at the apple and blackberry crumble on the sideboard. 'Save me some pudding.'

* * *

The long, winding drive to Fitzwarren Hall reminded Jack of the last time he'd made the journey, only then it was in a taxi instead of his police car. Back then, he'd felt his usual unease at having to socialize with people he didn't know. This time, he was keen to speak to everyone on site. The rows of cypresses that had twinkled with festive lights and lanterns now seemed sinister, like the trees in the Fanghorn Forest of Middle-Earth. Jack had read the books a dozen times but he still hadn't unravelled the mystery of the Stranger and Gandalf the Grey. He wasn't unduly superstitious but everything about Fitzwarren Hall felt menacing — full of dark secrets and centuries-old conflicts. He feared he was allowing his imagination to take over and immediately refocused. He had a job to do and his brief contact with the Fitzwarren family told him it was going to be fraught with more obstacles than an SAS assault course.

On the night of the party, the golden-gravelled courtyard of the Hall had been graced with Bentleys, Rolls-Royces and the like. It was now crammed with hastily parked police vehicles. Two SOCO vans were sited close to the boathouse with white-suited officers coming and going like an army of ants. Jack and Bugsy were greeted by a grim-faced Beach who showed them in.

'Your detective constables are already here, sir, and waiting for you in the library.'

Bugsy had summoned as many of the team as he could contact and they had obviously spared no time in getting there, despite it being Sunday.

'Where are the family members, Mr Beach?' asked Jack. 'We'll need to speak to everyone in the household and my officers will take their statements.'

'The Dowager Lady Beatrice has been taken away to the Richington Private Care Hospital by ambulance, sir. She suffered a severe cardiac incident but I am told she is expected to recover. At present she is under sedation and Sir Leonard Montgomery is with her. As for the rest of the family, I'm unsure who's in residence but I will find out for you, sir.'

'I believe you were first on the scene after Lady Beatrice found the body?' said Jack.

'That's correct, sir. Mrs Beach and I rushed to the boathouse when we got Lady Beatrice's cry for help. I administered CPR until the ambulance arrived. My wife phoned the police and they arrived soon after. Obviously, we made no attempt to interfere with the . . . er . . . body in the water although my wife recognized it as that of Lord Hugo.'

'We'll need a statement from you both but it can wait for now.' Jack could see that despite the poker-faced composure that went with his job, the man was shaken and no doubt his wife was, too. They needed time to come to terms with what had happened. At the moment, the man was functioning on automatic pilot.

The whole area around the boathouse was cordoned off by police tape and Police Constable 'Johnny' Johnson stood guarding the entrance with several of his uniformed colleagues. 'Nobody has entered or left since we got here, sir.'

'Thanks, Constable. I'm afraid you'll need to arrange with Sergeant Parsloe to be relieved as I suspect this is going to be a long job.'

'Yes, sir.' Johnny lifted the tape and Jack and Bugsy ducked underneath.

The Underwater and Confined Space Search Team, better known as the Met's Dive Team, specialised in situations such as this. They were searching the entrance to the boathouse and further out into the river, looking for any evidence that may have come adrift from the corpse.

'Someone has authorized a good deal of resource here,' Jack muttered to Bugsy.

'It won't have been Garwood,' Bugsy muttered back. 'Tighter than a duck's doodah when it comes to overtime and calling in specialist teams. I reckon the Commander's behind this.'

The pathologist, Doctor Veronica Hardacre, known covertly as Big Ron due to her formidable physique and even more formidable brain, was kneeling beside the rapidly disintegrating corpse. SOCOs had set up a temporary platform for her to work on.

She pulled down her mask when she spotted Jack. 'I suppose you know I've had to miss my Taekwondo class to come here, Inspector.'

Jack looked as apologetic as he could while trying to imagine her in a Taekwondo suit. On consideration, he decided it probably didn't look a lot different to her SOCO suit. 'Sorry, Doctor. I'll try to persuade murderers to be more considerate in future. Any initial thoughts?'

'I'll have a better idea when I've pieced him back together, but at the moment I'd say from the degree of decomposition, he's been dead in the water for a good month. When we removed the helmet, his head came with it. The muscles, ligaments and so on that hold the atlas joint have more or less dissolved or been eaten by something, allowing the head to come loose from the spine.'

'Gives a whole new meaning to losing your head,' quipped Bugsy.

Dr Hardacre gave him a withering look. 'I can do without gallows humour when I'm crawling about in disintegrating body parts, Sergeant.'

'Sorry, Doc.' Bugsy was curious. 'What kind of predator would have eaten bits of him in the Thames?'

'I'm a pathologist, Sergeant, not an aquatic biologist. Freshwater ecosystems are not within my remit. But the body has been down there long enough for a number of creatures to have had a meal.'

'A month would tally with the length of time he's been missing.' Jack rubbed his nose, pensively. 'Did he die here or somewhere else and his body was brought here and dumped?'

She shook her head. 'Impossible to tell at the moment. Work on the assumption that it could be either, until I've got him back on the slab.' She looked puzzled. 'Do you know why he was wearing the helmet from a suit of armour?'

'Not a clue. Lord Hugo comes from a somewhat eccentric family so your guess is as good as mine. But one thing I can promise — I shall find out.'

* * *

Unable to find anyone to direct them, Jack and Bugsy did several detours of the huge, labyrinthine property before they located the library. First, they stumbled on the family vault, with tombs bearing the recumbent marble effigies of long dead Barons Fitzwarren in full armour. Then they blundered into the billiard room and scared the daylights out of a maid polishing the balls. Knowing Bugsy's bawdy sense of humour, Jack knew he wouldn't be able to resist some sort of coarse comment and forestalled him.

'Don't even think about it, Sergeant.'

Bugsy grinned. 'As if I would, guv.'

The maid obligingly escorted them to the library where the four detective constables were waiting. Jack was pleased to see that they had been given tea and biscuits.

'Thanks for coming in so promptly, folks, especially on your day off. You'll be relieved to hear that we've located most of Lord Hugo's body in the boathouse.'

'That butler chap, Mr Beach, has filled us in with what he knows, sir. Where do you want us to start?' DC 'Chippy' Chippendale was still very new to the team and as always, keen to get working.

'The optimum time for investigating a murder is in the first twenty-four hours after it happens but, in this case, the pathologist says the deceased has been dead for best part of a month so we're already starting on the back foot. Add to that the size of this place, the number of people who will have been coming and going during that time and what I anticipate will be an uncooperative family and it's going to be uphill work.'

'Why do you anticipate resistance from the family, sir?' asked DC Williams. 'Surely they'll be anxious to find out what happened here.'

'In most cases, I'd agree, Aled, but this isn't a normal family.'

Bugsy helped himself to a chocolate hob-nob. 'What the boss means is that there's a strong undercurrent of silence. Unspoken warnings and shifty glances between them if it looks like one of them is about to let a dodgy cat out of the bag — and that was even before his nibs got the chop.'

'I don't suppose it could have been an accident, could it, sir?' ventured Chippy.

'How do you work that out?' asked Gemma.

'Well, what if he was trying on the helmet, just for fun, like you do, but because he couldn't see properly through the slits, he overbalanced with the weight on his head and fell in the water and drowned?'

'Ok, son,' said Bugsy, 'assuming that's a possibility, how did he totter from the Great Hall all the way to the boathouse without falling down two flights of massive staircases, negotiating several long winding corridors and without anyone seeing him?'

'Maybe he carried the helmet and only put it on when he got to the boathouse,' Chippy suggested.

'Why?' asked Gemma, ever the pragmatist.

'They're an eccentric family,' said Chippy. 'Perhaps he was intending to drive the motorboat down the Thames, wearing the helmet like a figurehead, to draw attention to the fact that he belonged to a long line of powerful Norman noblemen.'

'People have done dafter things,' agreed Velma, thinking of Kate Winslet on the prow of the Titanic. 'Do we know for sure that the cause of death was drowning, sir?'.

'Not until Dr Hardacre has carried out the post-mortem,' said Jack. 'And until then, we mustn't jump to any conclusions or make up our own scenarios. To that end, I've called up a search team to go over every inch of the house and grounds looking for anything relevant. What I'd like you all to do is take statements from as many members of staff as you can. Mr Beach will identify them for you. Find out who was the last person to see Lord Hugo alive and when and where they saw him. Then we'll draw up a timeline between then and when he was found dead. Start with the Beaches and try not to get lost. Sergeant Malone and I will question the family.'

That would have been Jack's next move except Beach came to report that not one of the family was currently in residence. As ever, he delivered the information with a completely dispassionate expression.

'Lady Helena has been informed of His Lordship's death and is staying with a friend for support, sir, but I'm not sure who or where. The Honourable Rupert spent the night in town and has failed to notify his current whereabouts or when he will return. His wife, Lady Louise is staying in the flat above the Fitz Gallery and Lady Charlotte is in the Cotswolds on the Fitzwarren Farm. And as you know, the Dowager Lady Beatrice is in hospital, being treated for a heart attack. Sir Leonard has stated that she is not yet well enough to be questioned.'

'But they do all know that Lord Hugo is dead?' asked Jack.

'Oh yes, sir. I took the liberty of notifying Mr Mackintosh, the family's solicitor, and he said he would take care of everything.'

'Thank you, Mr Beach. I must apologize in advance for the disruption to your household which will soon have a large number of police officers in uniform going over it. And, as I mentioned before, my detectives will also need to take statements from you and Mrs Beach, please.'

'Yes, of course, sir. My wife is still in shock but we will cooperate fully with anything you need.'

* * *

Jessie Beach sat at her kitchen table with a strong cup of tea to which Bob had added a nip of brandy. She was desperately trying to make sense of everything that had happened. As senior members of the household staff, she and Bob knew most of what went on in the family, but neither of them had seen this coming. His Lordship had been acting a little strangely of late but Bob had put it down to concerns about money and continuing to maintain Fitzwarren Hall. Jessie thought it was more than that. She had noticed the covert phone calls, made in his study, which had stopped abruptly whenever she entered to tend to the fire. Jessie believed that whatever had been worrying Lord Hugo prior to his murder had more to do with personal affairs than money.

* * *

'Looks like it'll have to be tomorrow before we can speak to the relatives,' said Bugsy.

'OK but let's take another look at the crime scene before we call it a day.' Jack wanted a closer look, now that Dr Hardacre, the mortuary assistants and the SOCO team had finally cleared up and taken away everything that was relevant. Because of the awkwardness of the location and the part the river had played, it had been a long-drawn-out and complicated process.

'Will there be anything left to see?' asked Bugsy.

'Probably not but I'd like to get a feel for how the whole thing might have panned out, what would have been possible for the murderer to accomplish and where he or she might have had to improvise.'

'OK guv. Whatever you say.' Although Bugsy had worked alongside Jack for years, he never failed to wonder at the depth of detail the inspector went into when he was reconstructing a murder.

The boathouse was very cold. The two motorboats were still bobbing on their pilings having been thoroughly examined by the SOCOs. Apparently, it had not been deemed necessary to tow them away for further exploration. Jack guessed this was because they had found no evidence of Lord Hugo having been on board when he was murdered.

'What are we looking for, guv?' Bugsy could feel the cold seeping through his lightweight jacket. He'd been dressed for Sunday lunch, not for hanging about in a draughty boathouse.

Jack was down on his hands and knees looking at something on the walkway. 'We have to accept that the crime scene has been contaminated by Mr and Mrs Beach who needed to get Beatrice Fitzwarren out of the boat and fast. If they hadn't, she'd probably have died here and there would have been two bodies to deal with. As a consequence, there are multiple foot prints all over the wet boards, not least the ambulance people who took her away. That doesn't help us find out whether Hugo died here or if he was killed somewhere else and his body dragged here later and chucked in.'

'And we're no closer to finding out the significance of the helmet,' added Bugsy.

'Let's hope the post-mortem gives us something to work with.' Jack noticed Bugsy shiver. 'Come on, time we went home. There's a dish of blackberry and apple crumble with my name on it.'

CHAPTER SIX

Bright and early on a crisp Monday morning and with a new murder case to work on, the MIT incident room of Richington nick was full. Detectives, legal support clerks, technical experts and archivists had all turned out to assist with the investigation. The whiteboard, however, was blank except for the photograph of Lord Hugo Fitzwarren in all his regalia.

'OK team, what have we got?' Jack looked around the room for contributions.

Aled stepped forward to the whiteboard. 'After we'd questioned the staff, a few of us went down to the Richington Taj Mahal for a curry and pooled our information.' He began to write. 'In terms of a timeline, we don't have much that helps, sir.'

'That's mainly because everybody we spoke to reported exactly the same time frame for the last time they saw Lord Hugo alive and nothing since,' added Gemma. 'That alone was suspicious.'

'The last sighting was at eight o'clock when the chauffeur, Carson, says he drove Hugo home in the Bentley from his office, which is confirmed by the CCTV footage,' said Chippy. 'We saw him going inside but never coming out again.'

'We took statements from every member of staff but nobody saw him after that night,' concluded Velma. 'The cook says he didn't request dinner so she assumed he'd already eaten and she went home. The maid who took him his early morning tea at seven-thirty next day as usual, said his bed hadn't been slept in so she took it away again.'

'Didn't she mention it to anyone?' asked Bugsy.

'No. Apparently the staff weren't in the habit of questioning the comings and goings of the family. In fact, they were actively discouraged,' replied Velma. 'Helena and Rupert frequently stayed out all night, and Charlotte often stayed on the farm so it wasn't unusual for a member of the family not to have slept in their bed.'

'So we're left with the working assumption that Hugo was murdered between eight o'clock that night and seven-thirty next morning when the maid went in with the tea.' Jack furrowed his brow, concentrating. 'What I can't work out is why nobody mentioned he was missing until Lady Charlotte reported it over a week later.'

Aled wrote what they knew on the whiteboard. 'Maybe you'll find out more when you speak to the family, sir.'

'I wouldn't bank on it, Aled. Those people can talk to you without saying anything. What about Lord Hugo's phone and laptop?' asked Jack. 'I understand the search team found them in his study.'

'Nothing on either that you wouldn't expect to find,' reported Clive. 'Just general day-to-day stuff, business emails back and forth to Napier-Smythe, messages to his personal assistant in his office, calls to Beach and Carson. I checked his personal bank account and again, nothing unusual except there wasn't much cash in it, which is odd for someone in his position. No large withdrawals or deposits. Unlike Lady Helena and the Honourable Rupert who spent money like water, or in Helena's case, like champagne. Their personal accounts were regularly emptied almost as soon as their allowances went in, never mind half a dozen maxed-out credit cards each.'

'Nice work if you can get it,' observed Aled, whose only credit card had started to wince whenever he took it out of his wallet.

'And all activity by Hugo ceased abruptly the night he disappeared.' Clive paused. 'It's strange that I didn't find any personal stuff, like calls to check in with his wife and mother. It suggests that he might have had another phone that we haven't traced.'

'Good point, Clive. I'd have thought he would at least have spoken to his old mum,' said Bugsy.

'Might I suggest that Jamie Mackintosh, the family solicitor, might be a person of interest, sir?' Velma offered.

'Why do you say that, DC Dinkley?' asked Jack. Velma's observations were always worth attention because she had a mindset that identified deeper motivations behind people's actions than the obvious ones.

'I took Mr Beach's statement, sir, and he reported that in the days before Lord Hugo went missing, Mackintosh had visited the house much more frequently than was normal. He would have noticed because as chief of staff, he would have opened the door to him each time. He also mentioned that Lord Hugo had seemed distracted after these visits and tended to hit the whiskey decanter quite hard. Beach wouldn't speculate but I got the impression he suspected more than he was letting on. As the consummate butler, he's the three wise monkeys rolled into one.'

'Thank you for that, Velma. I had Mackintosh on my list of people to question. I shall pay extra attention to his answers.' Jack made a mental note.

'I found no calls on his phone to Jamie Macintosh, either,' added Clive, 'which is odd considering how frequently he was visiting. There has to be another phone somewhere.'

Jack recalled the Commander telling him how Lord Hugo had been discussing a number of important issues with his lawyers and instructing them to draw up certain papers. But before he could sign anything, the bloke goes missing and ends up dead. Coincidence? Jack didn't think so. There had to be a connection. He threw it open to the team. 'Any initial thoughts, folks?'

'What kind of life events drive a bloke to hit the bottle?' prompted Aled. He prepared to write suggestions on the whiteboard.

'Money worries,' shouted someone. 'Sounds like his wife and son got through a fair bit of it.'

'Relationship issues,' called an admin clerk, who had plenty of his own. 'My wife has bought a chihuahua, despite my objections. It's a snappy, smelly little perisher. She's trained it to pee in my slippers.'

'Health problems,' said one of the older men. 'Maybe he had a dodgy prostate — that can be a real bugger. Not that whiskey would have helped. I know a bloke who had to go to hospital and a lady doctor put her finger up his . . .'

'OK, thanks,' said Jack, cutting him off before he went into the grisly details. 'Any initial suggestions as to who bumped him off?'

'I reckon the butler did it!' muttered someone. There were groans.

'Whoever said that pays for cream cakes,' declared Bugsy.

* * *

It was mid-afternoon before Dr Hardacre summoned Jack and Bugsy to witness the results of the post-mortem.

'Sorry for the delay, Inspector. I am aware that decomposition proceeds rapidly after a body is removed from the water and for that reason, the post-mortem should not be delayed but I have spent the morning extracting a chainsaw blade from a tree surgeon's chest. They really shouldn't let men have anything sharp.' She uncovered the examination table where the foetid remains of Lord Hugo Fitzwarren were pieced together in some kind of order but with much of it missing. 'This is all we could find of the late baron but it does tell us something of interest.'

'Like what, Doc?' asked Bugsy, who could only see a collection of slimy body parts, some of which seemed to have been eaten away by whatever wildlife lurked in the Thames.

'Firstly, we undertook a thorough investigation of the scene to determine if the location of the murder and the place where the body was recovered were the same.'

'And were they?' Jack was fighting back the waves of nausea that always affected him at post mortems, regardless of how gruesome the remains were. It was something to do with the antiseptic smells and the cold, clammy atmosphere.

She wrinkled her brow. 'In my opinion, yes — and no. I believe an attempted murder occurred on land and the body was subsequently placed in the water as a means of disposal.'

'And a bloody good one as it turned out,' said Bugsy. 'The bloke wasn't found for nearly a month. Might have been even longer if the old Dowager hadn't decided to take out one of the boats.'

'So the cause of death wasn't drowning?' asked Jack.

'As I said, yes and no.' She directed them to a screen on the mortuary wall showing Lord Hugo's skull from various angles. 'If you look at the damage to the back of the skull, you will see that this man had sustained blunt force trauma which would have been sufficient to render him unconscious.' She pointed to the spherical shape of the indented fracture.

'But was he still breathing?' asked Bugsy.

'I found fluid collections in what remained of the pleural cavities which may represent effusion as part of the drowning process. However, it isn't conclusive as I've known pleural fluid to be present in decomposing bodies irrespective of the cause of death.'

'But on balance of probabilities . . . ?' pressed Jack.

'On balance of probabilities, Inspector, I'd say that your killer bashed the deceased on the head with some kind of club or mace. I saw plenty to choose from in Fitzwarren Hall. We didn't find the weapon, so I assume the killer bleached off any blood and fingerprints and put it back on the wall.

Then the baron's head was forced into the armour helmet while he was unconscious but still alive. No fingerprints on the helmet, either, before you ask. His body was then shoved off the boardwalk and into the water where he stayed put. Without the weight of the helmet, he might have swelled up and floated under the gates of the boathouse and away down the Thames. For some reason, your killer wanted him to be found in situ.'

'Thank you, Doctor.' Jack turned to go. 'You've given us the 'how' 'where' and 'when'. All we have to do now is find out 'who' and 'why'.'

'Good luck with that,' she called after him.

* * *

'OK, folks, what do we think?' asked Jack. He looked hopefully around the incident room. Collectively, his troops had a good deal of wide-ranging knowledge and skills including the law, technology, psychology and sound common sense. DC Velma Dinkley was the first to speak. As a psychology graduate with first class honours, Velma looked more closely into the neurodiversity of suspects and their victims, which made her a valuable member of the team, especially when it came to behavioural analysis. Velma wasn't her real name. It was what Scooby Doo fans at university had called her and it had stuck, much to her mother's disappointment. As well as her undoubted intelligence, her collection of baggy sweaters and square glasses completed the characterization.

'I think the significance of the helmet is important, even though it's bizarre. It has two purposes in the mind of the killer — the practical one and the symbolic one. Practically, it ensures that if by some quirk of fate, Lord Hugo regains consciousness after the whack on the head, he'll die anyway because the weight will hold his head under water causing him to drown. Symbolically, it's mocking the wealthy peerage and the entitled aristocrats who still proudly display the trappings of their ancestors' victory in battle.'

'Right, Velma, so you reckon we're looking for a sub-versive, lefty pacifist who's handy with a mace,' said Bugsy.

'Do we think it's the same perp who stuck the knife in the painting?' asked Chippy.

'It's a thought, son,' said Bugsy. 'But defacing a painting is a long stretch from killing someone.'

'Sir, when you were at the birthday ball, did anyone test the dagger for fingerprints?' Aled wondered.

'No.' Jack recalled that nobody had thought of it in all the hullabaloo. 'It didn't seem necessary at the time. Nobody had been hurt and the only crime committed was damage to property. I expect Beach took it away and cleaned it with turps to get the red paint off.'

Before Jack could provide any further analysis, the door burst open and DCS Garwood strode in. 'Inspector Dawes, I need to speak to you.' He paused, his features twisting into a contorted look of pain. 'In my office, please.' He turned rapidly on his heel and hurried back out again with short, rapid steps as if his buttocks were clenched.

'Blimey, that was a quick visit,' observed Bugsy.

'Word in the canteen is that the Chief Super picked up a bad case of the trots while he was on holiday,' said Aled. 'He probably can't hang about anywhere for long.'

'So why didn't he just phone down and ask the Inspector to go to him, then?' asked Chippy.

'No, he wouldn't do that,' explained Gemma. 'He likes to appear in person every so often, just to make sure everyone knows he's the boss and he's still in charge.'

'It's the Napoleon Complex,' Velma pointed out. 'It's quite common in small men. How tall is he? Five-feet-seven? And Inspector Dawes is at least six-feet-three. Must be demoralizing, not to say a pain in the neck, having to look up all the time.'

'Next Christmas, we'll have a whip round and buy him some lifts for his shoes and a tall hat, like Brunel used to wear,' grinned Aled.

* * *

Chief Superintendent Garwood's office was pristine, having been buffed up by the cleaners every day that he was away. There'd been no one to fill the waste bin with rubbish every day or leave dirty cups and saucers on the desk. Nor did they find empty whiskey bottles behind the curtains. Jack tapped on the door and waited a few moments for Garwood's usual one word response — *Come*. He was about to knock again when Garwood emerged from his washroom down the corridor looking fragile.

'Ah, there you are, Dawes. About time. Come into my office, I need you to bring me up to speed with the Fitzwarren case.' They sat on opposite sides of Garwood's extravagant desk and there was a pause while he took out a blister pack of pills and swallowed a few. 'Sir Barnaby has been on the phone this morning, asking how close we are to arresting the killer.'

'Not very, I'm afraid, sir. We have established a number of facts surrounding Lord Hugo's death but we don't have any suspects yet.'

'Well, get a move on, man! We're dealing with an old and much-respected family. There have been Fitzwarrens in Kings Richington for donkey's years. They can trace their bloodline right back to—'

'The Battle of Hastings. Yes sir, so I've been told. Unfortunately, that doesn't help with finding out who wanted Lord Hugo dead or why they stuck a medieval helmet on his head. I have been unable to interview any of his relatives as they seem to have left the Hall without saying where they were going, but my team is busy tracking them down. The Dowager Lady Beatrice who found her son's body isn't out of danger yet and is too ill to be interviewed at present. In the meantime, my next move is to obtain a warrant and speak to the family's solicitors.'

'Ah yes. Mackintosh & Mackintosh. The Commander is an old friend of the semi-retired senior partner, Angus Mackintosh, so tread carefully, Dawes.'

'Of course, sir. I understand Lord Hugo was engaged in various negotiations with his lawyers before he went missing so I'm hopeful it will give us a lead.'

'Well, keep me in the loop.' He stood up. The pained expression returned. 'That will be all.' He followed Jack out into the corridor then darted back into his washroom.

* * *

When Jack got home after a long, frustrating day, he found Corrie in the kitchen preparing supper. The spicy aroma was intoxicating. He kissed her cheek. 'That smells good, sweetheart. What are we having?'

'Chicken Balti, keema naan and garlic and coriander rice.' Without looking up, she kissed the air beside his cheek and carried on stirring.

He guessed her day had been as tiring as his. 'Can I help you with that, darling? I'm sure I've made curry before.'

'Yes, I remember. You got 'tablespoon' and 'teaspoon' mixed up. It was so hot we could hardly eat it.'

'It wasn't my fault. The recipe was in very small print, 'tsp' and 'tbs' look very similar.' He dipped a finger in the sauce and sucked it. 'I read somewhere that curry's very good for you — lowers your cholesterol and blood pressure.'

'Yours wasn't inside us long enough for any health benefits. If I recall, it went straight through with barely a pause.'

'Bit like Garwood at the moment,' said Jack, getting a cold beer from the fridge. 'I don't know why he insists on coming into the office. He'd be much more comfortable at home.'

'Two reasons,' replied Corrie. 'Cynthia complains that when he's home, she can never get into the bathroom. I did point out that they have three, but she says you wouldn't want to use any of them after George has been in there, despite the industrial strength air freshener. And second, Sir Barnaby is leaning on him to get a grip and crack the Fitzwarren murder and he can't do that from home.'

'Frankly, my troops are working their arses off,' protested Jack. 'It doesn't make any difference if Garwood's there or not. I mean, does Sir Barnaby want us to catch the real murderer or will anybody do?'

'I can see your point. There's a snippet of gossip going round amongst some of the older ladies in Cyn's Luncheon Club that Dowager Beatrice knows more than she's letting on, but while she's still suffering the after effects of a heart attack, I suppose you can't question her.'

'No, and she has her guard dog, Sir Leonard, watching over her every minute so it'll be a while before I can speak to her.' He forked up some curry. 'This is amazing. Are there any poppadoms?'

CHAPTER SEVEN

The plush offices of Mackintosh & Mackintosh Law Firm in the centre of London's Chancery Lane legal quarter were a reflection of their extensive and lucrative practice. Clive had done a preliminary investigation and found that they acted for most of the affluent companies in the area. Jack had an appointment with Jamie Mackintosh at three but at three-thirty, he was still sitting in the elegant waiting room sipping weak tea provided by the immaculate if po-faced receptionist.

Unbeknownst to Jack, the delay was because Jamie was in his father's office being given advice on how much information he was legally obliged to reveal to the police and what he should keep to himself. It was a skill Angus had learned during his years at the Home Office.

'But Dad, the police have got a warrant. I don't see how I can avoid telling them what they want to know.'

Angus Mackintosh was resolute. 'Look, laddie, the success of this law firm is based on confidentiality and assurance that we always put the clients' interests first. If we get a reputation for releasing sensitive information at the first provocation, we'll lose our most valuable business and you'll lose that Ferrari you have in the garage.'

'So what do I tell them? I can't lie.'

'No, you don't need to lie, Jamie. Just don't volunteer any more information than you have to. Your first responsibility is to your client — alive or dead. The most important thing to remember is which part of the late Lord Hugo's affairs to keep confidential at all costs — warrant or no warrant.'

Still far from confident, Jamie emerged from his office and shook Jack's hand, warmly. 'Inspector Dawes. I'm so sorry to keep you waiting. Business is particularly brisk at present and the sudden death of Lord Hugo has thrown up a lot of unscheduled issues.'

They went into his opulent inner sanctum and Jack handed over the warrant. Jamie glanced at it then placed it on his desk, leaned back in his leather chair and steepled his fingers. 'My paralegal tells me that you need some information about the late Lord Hugo's circumstances before he died. Such a terrible business. I do hope I can be of some assistance in catching his killer, but I'm not sure I can tell you anything that you don't already know.'

Jack took that to mean that he probably could, but he wasn't going to. 'I understand from the staff of Fitzwarren Hall that you had been visiting Lord Hugo more frequently of late.' Jack chose his words carefully — the Fitzwarrens were a secretive bunch and he didn't want anyone losing their job for 'grassing' to the cops. 'Perhaps you could tell me why that was?'

'Nothing at all sinister, I can assure you. Mostly about day-to-day expenses.' He opened a file on his desk which surprised Jack as he imagined everything financial would have been kept encrypted online. 'Lord Hugo wanted the allowance that the estate made to his mother to be increased. As he pointed out, everything seems to cost so much more these days and she shouldn't have to penny-pinch in her old age. And he asked me to look at Fitzwarren Farm to see if the tax pressures could be reduced on the money obtained from breeding with the rare stock. There were a few other minor matters concerning the viability of donations to various charities, but sadly he died before he could sign any of those documents.'

'Nothing that might provide someone with a motive for wanting him out of the way, then?'

'No, Inspector, nothing like that at all. As I understand it from the editorial in the *Richington Echo*, the popular view is that he was murdered by some mentally ill extremist with a grudge against the aristocracy and strong views about the unfair distribution of wealth.'

Privately, Jack thought there was much more to it than a case of unhinged class envy. He was convinced that Mackintosh wasn't telling him everything, despite his legal duty. He made a mental note that when he got back to the office, he'd give Clive permission to do one of his surreptitious hacks to see if he could dig up the real reasons Hugo had been consulting his solicitor so frequently. In the meantime, he was handed Lord Hugo's file which contained exactly what Mackintosh said it did and nothing more. He continued to probe. 'The Fitzwarrens' butler, Mr Beach, told me that you had the unenviable task of notifying the family of the very sad news.'

'That's true.' The lawyer assumed an appropriately sombre expression. 'Not a duty that I relished, as you can imagine.'

'Would it be possible for you to give me some idea of how they reacted?'

Mackintosh looked surprised. 'That's an odd question, Inspector. I'm not sure what you want me to say. They reacted exactly how you would expect a close-knit family to react on hearing that the head of that family had suddenly been taken from them. Naturally, Lady Helena was devastated. It was a terrible shock.'

'Do you know where she is now? Mr Beach said she had gone to stay with a friend for support but she isn't answering her phone.'

'Poor Helena, she simply couldn't bear to stay at Fitzwarren Hall without Hugo. It was too painful so she reached out to a friend for comfort.'

'Do you have a name or contact details for this friend?' Jack asked more in hope than expectation.

'No, I'm afraid not. Lady Helena has requested that her privacy is respected at this very difficult time but obviously all our thoughts are with her and the rest of the family.'

Jack had never understood how 'thoughts' could be 'with' anyone other than the person who was thinking them, but it was what random people trotted out when they wanted to appear sympathetic. And 'respecting her privacy' simply meant she didn't want anyone asking any inquisitive questions. 'What about the son?' Jack wondered why Helena hadn't 'reached out' to her children for comfort.

'I understand that the Honourable Rupert — or should I say the 28th Baron of Richington as he is now — is staying at one of his clubs in town but—'

'You don't know which one,' finished Jack.

'Correct. His wife, Lady Louise, was in the flat above the Fitz Gallery when I last spoke to her, but I think she mentioned something about going home to Scotland to stay with her parents until the funeral. I'm assuming the police will let us know when the . . . er . . . body . . . is to be released and a funeral can be arranged. The Honourable Charlotte is staying on the family farm. She was very upset and said being with the animals would give her solace. I can give you the phone number of the farm, if that would help.'

'Thank you but I think I might pay her a visit.' Jack knew when he was being fobbed off but he sure as hell didn't know why. 'If anything else should occur to you, Mr Mackintosh—' *Jack was pretty sure that it wouldn't* — 'please give me a call.'

* * *

After Jack left, Angus came out of his office to speak to Jamie. 'How did it go, son?'

He pursed his lips. 'OK, I think. There was only one tricky moment when he asked if I knew of anything that might provide someone with a motive for wanting Lord

Hugo out of the way. After the kind of work he'd asked me to do, I reckon it could have been any of them.'

* * *

Jack could have asked the local police to interview Charlotte at Fitzwarren Farm but felt she would be more forthcoming with a familiar face. He took DC Fox with him thinking that Charlotte might relate better to a female officer. They chatted on the journey along the M4 until they reached the honey-coloured stone cottages and nodding hellebores of the Cotswolds.

'What did you make of the staff at Fitzwarren Hall, Gemma? Did anyone stand out as especially hostile to Lord Hugo?'

'Not really, sir. Half of them, like the gardeners and the part-time employees, didn't see much of him. Everyone else reckoned he was OK and couldn't think of a reason why anyone would want to kill him. They were fairly tight-lipped about his relationship with his wife, though, and I noticed that their bedrooms were on opposite sides of the house.'

'That's interesting. The family solicitor told me Lady Helena was devastated and wanted the police to respect her privacy while she grieved.'

'Another thing I thought was odd. The family motto *Nemini Confidite* was on a plaque above the door of the Great Hall. Mr Beach said Lord Hugo had told him it meant *Name of Confidence* and referred to the faith people had in the Fitzwarrens.'

'Why is that odd, Gemma? It's the kind of motto you'd expect, given how proud the baron was of his lineage.'

'I learned some Latin when I was studying for my law degree — things like *prima facie* and *sub judice*. I know my Latin's a little rusty now but I'm pretty sure *Nemini Confidite* means *Trust No One.*'

'Is that right?' Jack was still pondering on the signifi-cance of that as they drove through the open five-bar-gate into Fitzwarren Farm. DC Chippendale had phoned ahead so the estate manager, Adam Baker, was waiting for them.

Jack produced his ID. 'I'm Detective Inspector Dawes and this is my colleague, DC Fox. Thank you for agreeing to see us, Mr Baker.'

Adam, a man of few words, nodded and led them into the warm farmhouse kitchen where his daughter, Danielle, and Lady Charlotte were drinking coffee and eating lemon drizzle cake. 'Dani, give the officers some coffee and cake. I need to feed the pigs.' He hurried out.

Danielle stood up. 'You've come to speak to Charlie, haven't you? Would you like to go through to the lounge?'

Jack reckoned her to be around the same age as Charlotte and their obvious mutual love of animals clearly made them close friends. 'No, the kitchen's fine. We can chat here. Please don't leave, Miss Baker. I'm sure Charlie would like some support.'

Charlie was pale and her eyes were sunken and red-rimmed. She had clearly taken the murder of her father very hard. 'What do you want me to tell you, Inspector. I'll do anything I can to help catch whoever did this terrible thing to Pa.'

'Can you tell me when you last saw your father?'

'Well, it would have been the night before he went missing, wouldn't it?' She was surprised at such an obvious question. 'Nobody saw him after that — except the killer, of course. Carson drove Pa home in the Bentley and he came to say goodnight.'

'How did he seem?'

She thought about this. 'It seems a long time ago now but I don't remember anything in particular except . . .' She hesitated. 'When he was leaving my room, he turned back and said, 'Whatever I might say or do over the next few weeks, Charlie, never forget that I love you.' That was a bit odd, don't you think? He was tired and a bit distant but then he'd been working late. I think business must have been on his mind.' She paused, wondering if she should continue.

'I guess I should tell you about some things that happened those times when Pa was here on the farm.'

'What things would those be, miss?' probed Jack.

Charlie hesitated again, remembering how her father had stopped her from speaking up when the Inspector had asked if there had been any incidents before the damage to the painting. Well, it couldn't hurt now, could it? And it might help catch his killer. 'One of the barns caught fire while Pa was in there, getting bedding for some rare new lambs. He only just got out in time because the sliding door jammed. But it was an accident. An electrical fault or a stray match on a bale of hay. Something like that. And then there was that time the quad bike he was riding caught fire.'

'Really?' Gemma was writing it all down.

'But that was an accident, too. He didn't see the sparks in time and the extinguisher was missing.' She turned to Jack. 'You don't think those incidents have anything to do with his murder, do you?'

'I really can't say at present, miss, but I'll need to look into it.' He turned to Gemma who had been unusually quiet. 'Do you have any questions, DC Fox?'

'Might it be possible for me to have a look around the farm? I'd really like to see some of the rare breeds while I'm here.'

Both Charlie and Dani jumped up, keen to show Gemma round. Jack guessed there were questions Gemma wanted to ask that she felt might be better received without him there. He went and had a few words with Adam Baker but had to accept that it was unlikely he could contribute much as he had little direct contact with Hugo or Fitzwarren Hall, except financially. He was dedicated to the farm and Jack thought that together with Charlie and Dani and the rest of the workers, the rare breeds couldn't be in safer hands. But he wondered what would happen now that the dashing Lord Rupert was in control.

Driving back to the station, Jack asked if Gemma had uncovered anything useful.

'I learned that Golden Guernsey Goats are rare but showing stability and the Gloucester Old Spot pig is still at risk. But I'm guessing you mean the case, sir. The main thing I picked up was what we already know — the whole Fitzwarren dynasty is dysfunctional. Charlie believes that ever since she and Rupert were small, there has been some shameful family secret that they all know about but that her father forbade anyone to mention, including Dowager Beatrice. She said if we could get to the bottom of that, we would find the killer because she's sure that's at the back of it.'

'In the meantime, it's Rupert, the heir to the title, who will rule the roost and it's anyone's guess how that will turn out.' Jack braked to allow a rabbit to scurry across the road. 'It's good that Charlie has a friend in Danielle as I think the future could be difficult for a while.'

Gemma hesitated. 'I think Charlie and Dani are rather more than friends. Did you notice their necklaces, sir?'

'No. What about them?'

'They are two halves of a gold heart, split down the middle and engraved 'keeper of my heart'. They each wear one half on a chain. Apparently, Charlie has wanted to move out of Fitzwarren Hall and onto the farm with her partner for a long time but her father was dead against it. Something about the honour of the Fitzwarrens.'

'It's a very foolish man who puts some misplaced allegiance to a family name before the happiness of his daughter.'

'That's what I thought, sir. Anyway, she's going to do it, now that there's nothing stopping her.'

Privately, Jack wondered whether Lord Hugo's Will would have any bearing on the subject and at the same time, he realized that was why Gemma was so good on these occasions as she noticed things that he didn't.

CHAPTER EIGHT

'Jack, there's some mud stuck to your shoes and you're walking it all over the kitchen floor.' Corrie was following him around with a dustpan and brush.

'Sorry, darling. I expect I picked it up on Fitzwarren Farm. DC Fox and I went there to interview Charlotte, Lord Hugo's daughter.'

'So it's probably manure I'm sweeping up.' She wrinkled her nose in distaste.

'Yes, but it's a better class of manure than your average cow muck. The farm specializes in rare breeds.'

'Well, it still smells as bad. For goodness sake, take off your shoes.'

Jack sat on a kitchen chair and untied his laces. 'From what Charlotte told me, it seems that there were a couple of half-hearted attempts on Lord Hugo's life before the killer finally finished the job.'

'Really?' Corrie was intrigued. 'Why didn't he report it to the police?'

'I guess because he didn't want anything to reflect badly on the family.'

'Sounds just like my mother,' recalled Corrie. 'Whenever I hurt myself doing something daft, her immediate reaction was never, *Are you all right, Corrie?* It was always, *Oh, Coriander, what will people think?* I doubt if any kind of validation ever crossed her mind. I guess poor Charlotte doesn't have much of a loving role model in her mother, either.'

'Why do you say that?' Jack was all ears.

'According to Cynthia Garwood, Lady Helena has been having extra-marital . . . whatsname. You know . . . hanky-panky.'

Jack grinned. 'Do you mean a bit on the side?'

'More than a bit, apparently. Quite a lot. And Hugo knew but wouldn't do anything about it because—'

'*What will people think?*' finished Jack.

'Exactly. Cynthia reckons Helena's current dalliance is Dickie Napier-Smythe.'

'Wasn't he the late Lord Hugo's business partner?' Jack was sensing a connection and now he had a pretty good idea who the 'friend' was that she had 'reached out' to in her 'grief'. He really needed to ask Lady Helena a few pointed questions about how much Lord Hugo knew about the liaison.

'That's right,' said Corrie. 'But I suppose it doesn't matter what she does or who she does it with, now that she's a widow.'

Jack pondered. 'It does rather beg the question of what's in the Will, though.' When he'd asked Jamie Mackintosh how long it would be before he would be reading it to the family, he'd waffled something about a very complicated probate and how it could take some time. Jack decided that in addition to delving into Mackintosh & Mackintosh Law Firm, he would get Clive to look into the affairs of Fitzwarren & Napier-Smythe Asset Management. It would be helpful to know the extent of Hugo's personal assets and if there was any life insurance.

* * *

The investigation trundled on without any significant breakthrough. On the principle that excrement rolls downhill, the local MP was leaning on the Commander who was leaning on DCS Garwood who in turn was leaning on Jack.

'It reflects badly on the entire service, Dawes. An important member of the community, and a baron to boot, is murdered in cold blood on our patch and here we are, some weeks later, and no closer to catching the killer. What are you doing about it, man? The Commander is threatening to bring in a Special Task Force from HQ and you know what that means. The whole investigation will go tits-up, the murderer will scarper to somewhere exotic and out of reach and my budget will be cut.'

Jack knew exactly what Garwood meant. The last time it happened was when there had been a spate of burglaries in the area and the Commander's family silver was stolen, along with Lady Lobelia's jewellery. Sir Barnaby had called in a 'Special Task Force' who worked on the case for six weeks during which time they managed to piss off everyone in the nick including the easy-going Sergeant Parsloe. Finally, completely baffled, they put in a report saying that the loot must have been fenced abroad, then filed colossal expense and overtime claims before pushing off back to HQ. Next day, a uniformed constable cycling home from a football match spotted the entire haul in the window of a pawn shop.

Jack played for time. 'We are following a number of new leads, sir. I'm confident there'll be some progress very soon.' His fingers were firmly crossed.

* * *

Efforts to find Lady Helena were hampered by the fact that she didn't want to be found. Mackintosh insisted that he didn't know her whereabouts and in any case he reiterated her right for her privacy to be respected. After what Corrie had told him about Helena's unashamed reputation for hanky-panky, Jack thought she had forfeited any right to privacy by falsely claiming she was prostrate with grief. It was then he remembered Corrie telling him what Cynthia had said about Helena's visits to Napier-Smythe's cabin cruiser and how they probably weren't discussing stocks and shares. Naturally, Jack didn't approve of gossip but it didn't half come in useful sometimes and was often the lifeblood that ran through the veins of successful detective work.

'Bugsy, how do you fancy a visit to a cabin cruiser on the St Katharine's Dock marina?'

'Not much, guv. All that rising and falling and rocking about makes me ill. Just being in the Fitzwarrens' boathouse watching the motorboats bobbing up and down made me queasy.'

'OK. Aled, you're with me.' Jack thought Aled, young handsome and fit, would encourage more cooperation from Helena than a nauseous Bugsy.

Clive had tracked down the marina and checked that it was where Dickie kept his boat. When Jack and Aled arrived, they parked the police car out of sight and found the marina administrator who immediately went into sales mode.

'Good morning, gentlemen. Are you looking for a mooring for your yacht? We have one or two still available.'

They produced their ID. 'No thank you, tempting though it is.' Fleetingly, Jack wondered what it would be like to have a boat you could escape to and relax on long free weekends. Then he realized that it was very rare that either he or Corrie ever had a long free weekend, and certainly not at the same time, so it was pointless dreaming. 'Could you please lead us to this cabin cruiser?' He nodded to Aled who showed the man the details on his phone.

'Oh yes. That one belongs to Mr Napier-Smythe. I don't believe he is on board at present but his wife is. At least, I think the lady is his wife.' He escorted them to the mooring.

Aled shouted before they climbed down into the boat. 'Hello? This is the police. Anybody on board?' There was no answer but they could hear noises coming from the aft cabin. Jack called out. 'This is Detective Inspector Dawes and Detective Constable Williams. Can you come out, please?'

Helena emerged looking hung over and cross at being disturbed. She wore shortie peach silk pyjamas and a matching robe which she pulled tightly around her. 'What do you two want?' She tossed back her long blonde hair, now sleek and straight, instead of tied up in a bun as usual. 'If it's about Hugo, I don't know anything.'

So much for the grieving widow, thought Jack. He could see no sign of the devastation that Mackintosh had described but there was no doubt that she had 'reached out to a friend for comfort' and a good deal of champagne too, if the empty bottles were anything to go by.

'Just a few questions, Mrs Fitzwarren,' said Jack. 'Then we'll leave.'

'I don't have to answer your questions. Didn't Jamie Mackintosh tell you? And the correct form of address is Lady Fitzwarren.' She turned to go back into the cabin.

'Is Mr Napier-Smythe on board, madam?' Jack craned his neck, trying to peer inside the sleeping quarters.

'No, he's in his office in the city — not that it's any of your business.'

Aled turned on the Welsh charm, remembering what his Grannie Williams always said about *catching more flies with honey than with vinegar, cariad*. 'We're very sorry to distress you when you're obviously grieving, Lady Fitzwarren, but it's our job to find out who murdered your husband. We'll try to be as compassionate as we can if you could give us just a few minutes of your time. Then we'll leave you in peace to rest.'

Helena clocked Aled's muscular good looks and smiled for the first time, effectively ignoring Jack, who distanced himself by climbing off the boat, thinking Aled could manage this interview better without him. She indicated the seating area. 'You'd better sit down, Detective Williams. What is it you want to know?' She sat close to him, letting her wrap fall away slightly from her undeniably splendid figure.

'Can you think of a reason why anyone would want to harm your late husband?'

She shrugged. 'Not really. People don't usually get bumped off just for being boring, do they?'

'May I ask why you found him boring?'

She pulled a sour face. 'He was always going on about his precious ancestry — how he could trace the Fitzwarrens back almost a thousand years. I mean, who cares about that stuff these days? He used to say, "we weren't put on this earth to enjoy ourselves, Helena." Well, what the hell are we here for then? I bet you like to have a good time, don't you, officer?'

Aled smiled politely. 'What about Mr Napier-Smythe? How does he fit into the picture?'

'Dickie amused me when Hugo couldn't be bothered. I suppose you think that's awful of me.'

'We're not here to judge, my lady, just to get some facts.'

'Well, I fulfilled my purpose when Rupert was born. Hugo wanted a 28th Baron to carry on the line and I gave him one. After that, I considered myself free to do whatever I liked. Poor Lottie was a mistake, but she's happy enough mucking out and feeding the animals on the farm.' She took a bottle out of the small fridge. 'Champagne, officer?'

'No thank you, my lady. It's a bit early for me.'

'It's never too early for champagne, sweetie. Have you got a girlfriend?'

Aled thought it safer to ignore that. He opened the bottle for her, expertly, without letting it fizz over. He had learned the trick from a bar tender in Pontypool. 'Do you know if Lord Hugo had life insurance?'

She sighed. 'Now you're being boring, too. I haven't a clue if he had insurance. You'd need to ask Jamie. Why is everything always about money?'

Aled secretly thought that the only people who asked that were the ones who had access to loads of the stuff so it was never a problem. 'As far as you're aware, Lord Hugo didn't have any enemies — anybody with a grudge?'

'No. At least, not as many as his father.' She giggled. 'Old William Fitzwarren was a real terror and a drunk. I'm not surprised somebody put a knife through his portrait. The only mystery is why nobody put a knife through him when he was alive. I don't know how Beattie put up with him as long as she did. He had a terrible temper.' She emptied her glass and held it out for a refill.

'What about Lord Hugo's Will? Who gets Fitzwarren Hall and the rest of the estate?'

'I've no idea but I imagine we'll all be taken care of. Hugo wouldn't have wanted the scandal of relatives left in poverty after his death. And of course, my son, Rupert is next in line. No doubt his dippy wife Louise will whelp eventually, when she can be bothered.'

Aled eventually managed to extricate himself despite Helena's protestations that 'there's still oodles of champers left, darling'.

'Phew!' He joined Jack on dry land. 'I took one for the team there, sir.'

Jack grinned. 'You certainly did, Aled. Well done. What did you find out?'

'In a nutshell, she couldn't tell me if Lord Hugo had any enemies, she didn't know how the estate would be managed now he's dead but was sure everyone would be taken care of and since she'd provided an heir, Rupert, she felt she'd fulfilled her part of the contract and was entitled to do whatever she liked with whomever she liked.'

'And did you believe her?' asked Jack.

'Not really, sir, no. That lady knows exactly what she's doing, despite the frivolous flirty act. I think it's very unlikely she would just trust to luck how things would turn out. If she had the least suspicion that Lord Hugo might have been planning to cut her off without what she considers she's earned, she wouldn't have hesitated to put a stop to him.'

'Or persuade someone else to do it for her,' suggested Jack. 'Good work, Aled. I'm pretty sure Mackintosh isn't telling us everything, either. The answer could be there. And I think we should have a few words with Napier-Smythe.'

* * *

Clive had been delving deep into some databases that were probably out of bounds but the way he saw it, you can't make an omelette without breaking a few eggs. Eventually, he had something to report.

'Sir, there's something you need to see.'

'Clive, please tell me it's good news.'

'I managed to get into some of the databanks of Fitzwarren & Napier-Smythe Asset Management. Investments and hedge funds aren't really my field, sir, but I have a friend who works in finance and I asked him to take a look. He said that over the last year, investors' accounts have been systematically plundered and large sums of money have been moved into offshore banks. We're talking millions. He couldn't be more specific but he reckoned he'd seen something similar before and it turned out the person responsible had been preparing to do a runner once he had enough cash stashed away.'

'Good work, Clive.' Jack called the team together. 'Listen up, folks. It looks like before Lord Hugo went missing, he'd been cooking the books and stealing from his clients, ready to leg it abroad. He might have got away with it except someone found out and put a stop to him.'

Velma had that look on her face that told Jack she was doubtful. 'That doesn't sound in keeping with his Fitzwarren commitment to honour, sir. And I can't see him leaving Fitzwarren Hall and all the trappings of his ancestors.'

'You'd be surprised what people will do if enough cash is involved,' said Bugsy. His overriding approach to any investigation was always 'follow the money'.

'Well, there's one way to find out,' said Jack. 'We'll get the Serious Fraud people to investigate the company then pay Napier-Smythe a visit.'

CHAPTER NINE

'Guv, I just heard from the hospital.' Bugsy called to Jack across the incident room. 'Lady Beatrice has been allowed home. She's back in the Dower House.'

'Right.' Jack grabbed his coat. The weather had turned colder and there was even the threat of snow. 'Let's get over there and talk to her.'

'Sir, remember what Charlie told me out at the farm?' Gemma reminded him. 'She reckons there's some shameful family secret that her father had forbidden anyone to mention. She also said that if we could find out what it was, it would most probably lead us to the killer. Since the old Dowager has been around longer than any of them, it's my guess that she knows all about it. We just need to persuade her to tell us so we can catch whoever murdered her son.'

'Thanks, Gemma. We'll see what she has to say. The shock of finding bits of her son floating around the boathouse might have changed her mind about preserving the honour of the Fitzwarrens in favour of a more realistic reaction.'

* * *

The Dower House was covered in a light sprinkling of snow, as if someone had dusted it with icing sugar. The trees and shrubs in the well-maintained garden sparkled with frost and glistening networks of spiders' webs. It looked, Bugsy thought, like something from a fairy story, probably Hansel and Gretel, which had been his step-granddaughter Olivia's favourite when she was little. Bugsy wasn't prone to fantasy but he made an exception in the case of his inherited and much-loved grand-children and had spent hours reading to them. He spotted Sir Leonard Montague's racing-green Morgan parked outside with the roof up. Sensible, observed Bugsy. You wouldn't want to come out and find it full of snow. Or even worse, jump in without looking, then spend the rest of the day with a wet arse.

The Dowager's housekeeper opened the door to them and asked them to wait in the hall while she notified Her Ladyship. It was actually Sir Leonard who came out to speak to them.

'Lady Beatrice has said she will see you but please take it gently, officers, and don't stay too long. She's still very fragile and her heart isn't strong, even on a good day — and as you can imagine, this isn't a good day.'

They were shown into the Dowager's ornate bedroom where she was propped up on pillows and wearing a fluffy pink bedjacket. Her grey hair was tied up with ribbon and she had managed to put on some lipstick.

'Lady Beatrice,' began Jack, gently. 'How are you feeling?'

'A little better, thank you, although I'm not sure how I can help you. I understand Bob and Jessie Beach told you what happened and there isn't anything I can add.'

'As we understand it, you were going to take out one of the motorboats to visit Sir Leonard, when you found Lord Hugo's body floating in the boathouse.' Jack tried not to make it too graphic — yet.

She shuddered. 'Yes. It was horrible — ghastly. I was sick, then I had a searing pain in my chest and I don't remember anything much after that. They tell me dear Bob Beach saved my life.'

'Can you think of any reason why somebody would knock your son unconscious with a medieval mace, force the helmet from a suit of armour on his head and leave him in the boathouse to drown?' This time, Jack didn't hold back, thinking that if she was made to face the brutal reality, it might shock her into telling him what and who she suspected was behind it. It didn't.

'No!' she shrieked. 'It wasn't murder! It was a terrible accident! It must have been! Nobody wanted to harm my son. Everybody loved him.' Gasping, she snatched an inhaler from the bedside table and took a huge breath, then another.

'Really, Inspector.' Sir Leonard intervened. 'That was unnecessarily cruel.' Sir Leonard poured her a glass of water and sat beside her on the bed with his arm around her.

'I'm sorry but we have recently been given to understand that there had been one or two previous attempts on Lord Hugo's life. Also, that there was some incident or misdemeanour in the Fitzwarren family's past that could be the key to why Lord Hugo was murdered,' explained Jack. 'It may also be connected to the defaced portrait of the late Lord William. We have been told by a family member that Lady Beatrice may know what it is.'

Sir Leonard blustered. 'I'm sure that isn't true. I've known the Fitzwarren family for many years and I'm certain I'd be aware of anything of that nature.'

Yes, thought Bugsy, *and I'm equally certain you'd keep it to yourself*. Talk about closing ranks. These nobs were unbelievable. Why would you keep schtum about something that might enable the police to nail the person who'd bumped off someone you loved? After all, how shameful could this secret be? *One person's shame is another person's misspent youth.*

'Which family member told you?' demanded Beatrice, suddenly calm and calculating. 'Was it Helena? You shouldn't believe anything she says. The woman's a slut. She didn't deserve my son.'

Jack didn't comment. 'You're sure, Lady Beatrice, that you can't think of anything that might reflect badly on your family — enough for someone to want Lord Hugo dead?'

'No, I can't. Now go away and leave me alone.' She buried her face on Sir Leonard's chest. 'Monty, make them go away.'

Outside, Bugsy turned up his collar against the snow-flakes. 'Well, what did you make of that, guv?'

'Now I'm even more convinced that they're hiding something and the only person who'll talk to us — Charlie — doesn't know what it is. We just have to keep digging.'

* * *

Louise Fitzwarren had returned to the Hall to collect her belongings prior to leaving for good. After a tearful conversation with her parents in the Scottish Highlands, they had convinced her that she should come home. They were horrified and disgusted at the way their Lulu had been treated by the so-called English nobility. Her father even went so far as to bring up comparisons with 'Butcher Cumberland' at Culloden and the heavy hand of the vindictive English. He was a Fraser — a clan that had fought on the side of Bonnie Prince Charlie and had been slaughtered indiscriminately as a result. Her mother had believed that her Lulu had made a good marriage where she would be loved and looked after and eventually, she would provide her with lots of grandchildren. It was heartbreaking the way things had turned out and she wanted her back home as soon as possible.

Jack had asked Beach if he would let the police know when Rupert's wife returned to Fitzwarren Hall as he needed to ask her some questions. She and Rupert were the only members of the household yet to be questioned, not that he expected to get anything useful from either of them. It was Mrs Beach who made the call and pointed out that Lady Louise would be going back home to Scotland for good and as soon as possible, so if they needed to speak to her, it would have to be soon. She also mentioned that sadly, the poor lady was not in the best of health and indicated, delicately, that 'women's troubles' may be involved.

'DC Fox, DC Dinkley, can you take this one, please?' While Jack wasn't reluctant to confront such matters when necessary, he thought it would be kinder and more productive if Louise was questioned by two young women of a similar age, rather than two old buffers like himself and Bugsy.

Mrs Beach showed Gemma and Velma into one of the reception rooms and after a few minutes, Louise joined them.

'Hello. I believe you want to talk to me.'

Both officers thought Louise looked pale and unwell.

Gemma started. 'We're sorry to disturb you, Lady Louise . . .'

'Oh, please, drop the title. I shan't be a baron's wife for very much longer and I'm quite happy with Louise or even Lulu if you like. How can I help?'

This came as something of a surprise. It appeared that either Rupert or Louise was planning to divorce. Velma continued: 'As you know, it's the job of the police to find out who murdered your father-in-law, Lord Hugo. We're trying to get a picture of the events leading up to the crime.'

'The police might consider it a crime but I see it as karma. The man was a tin-pot little dictator — an obsessive bully and an unmitigated snob. What else is there to know?'

Gemma trod carefully. 'Are you aware of anything that took place in the Fitzwarrens' past that might now cast doubt on their integrity? Maybe some sort of grudge that has resurfaced?'

She chewed her lip, thinking. 'No, not really. There was that time a year or so ago when some money went missing and Hugo accused one of the maids. It got quite nasty until much later when Helena admitted she took it because she'd maxed out her credit card and she needed to get her nails done. But by then, the poor girl had been sacked and branded a thief and Hugo made no attempt to admit he was wrong and put things right. That's the sort of man he was.'

'We're thinking more of an incident that might have happened some years ago.'

'No, I don't think so and I doubt if Rupert knows of anything bad. If he had, he'd have used it to blackmail a more generous allowance out of his father.'

'Do you know where we can contact your husband?' asked Velma. 'We need to speak to him, too.'

'I've no idea where the bastard is and I don't care. He'll be with one of his tarts. From now on, I'll be contacting his solicitor through my solicitor and Rupert will be looking down the barrel of a very expensive settlement.'

Gemma probed. 'Do I take it that you are planning to divorce him?'

'Too bloody right I am and it's going to cost him! I was recruited to this family with the sole purpose of providing an heir — carrying on the cherished Fitzwarren line — and I was prepared to go along with that. I wanted babies of my own to look after.'

'How were you "recruited"?' asked Velma, thinking it was a strange choice of word for a betrothal.

'Hugo was in Scotland on financial business, something to do with shares in the sale of single malt whiskey and salmon to Japan. He saw me working in a nursery, looking after little ones and I guess he thought I'd be ideal — innocent, naïve and easily manipulated and far enough away not to have heard any gossip about the Fitzwarren family. He invited me down to London and Fitzwarren Hall to meet his son. I'd always wanted to see London, so I agreed like a fool. I don't know how he sold the idea of marriage to Rupert — an increased allowance, I guess.'

'Did you have a big, extravagant wedding, as you were marrying into the peerage?' asked Velma.

'Good heavens, no. It was all over in half an hour. It wasn't an occasion for celebration as far as the Fitzwarrens were concerned — it was the sealing of a contract. They didn't even invite my parents. It was simply a formality that had to take place in order to ensure the legitimacy of the next baron that I was supposed to produce. And I had to go through a physical examination before Hugo would allow the marriage to go ahead.'

'That's awful,' muttered Gemma. The already low opinion she had of this family plummeted even further.

'Anyway, my father-in-law got impatient when I didn't get pregnant after a couple of years so he sent me to a Harley

Street gynaecologist. Now I find out that Lord sodding Rupert's dirty tomcat habits have given me a filthy disease that has put paid to my ability to have children — ever.' Despite her anger, there were tears in her eyes. 'When I told Hugo about his precious son, he had the nerve to suggest that I had been unfaithful and caught it from a lover after we were married. He said I'd better leave before I infected Rupert. Well, there's no way I'm going without a fight and it's going to cost the Fitzwarrens money — a great deal of it. I don't know what this scandal is that you're talking about but I can assure you that soon, there's going to be a much bigger one!'

There didn't seem a lot more to be said so Gemma and Velma thanked her for her cooperation and left.

'What did you make of that?' asked Velma on the way back to the station.

'I felt sorry for her and it's reinforced my determination never to get married.'

'One thing's for sure. If she'd known of any skeletons in the Fitzwarren cupboard, she'd have told us, given the way she must be feeling about that family. It must have been something that happened before her time with them.'

* * *

While Gemma and Velma were getting the low down on yet another dismal aspect of the unusual family, Jack and Bugsy were at the offices of Fitzwarren & Napier-Smythe Asset Management where a young woman showed them straight into Napier-Smythe's office.

When Jack and Bugsy suggested there may be instances of malpractice and the Fraud Squad would be carrying out an audit, Napier-Smythe seemed genuinely shocked. Although, as Bugsy said afterwards, it was hard to tell whether that was because he had trusted his partner or he'd been complicit in the deception and didn't think the cops were on to them.

'It appears, sir, that before his death, Lord Hugo was planning to go abroad having stolen a great deal of investors' money.

Did you have any warning of these plans?' Jack watched his face for the slightest twitch of recognition but there wasn't one.

'No, officers, no indication at all. Obviously, I didn't check on his aspects of the business, because I had no reason to doubt his honesty. Far from it. He gave every impression that his personal probity was important to him.'

'What about Lady Helena Fitzwarren, sir? Do you think she knew?' Bugsy asked. 'We understand that you and she are . . . shall we say . . . close friends.'

This time he did register concern. 'Did she tell you that?'

'Well, are you involved with her or not, sir?' Bugsy insisted.

Napier-Smythe hesitated. 'I may have taken Lady Helena out to dinner a couple of times when Hugo was abroad on business. There's nothing sordid about that, as you appear to be trying to imply. I was merely ensuring she was looked after, as Hugo had requested.'

'When we spoke to her, she was on your cabin cruiser. She was wearing night clothes and gave every impression of having spent the night there. You must understand, Mr Napier-Smythe, we are investigating Lord Hugo's murder and that means speaking to everyone who may have had a motive.' Jack had touched a nerve.

'Are you suggesting I killed Hugo in order to make off with his wife? That's preposterous! I'd like you to leave now and make no mistake, I shall be lodging a formal complaint with your senior officer.'

'That, guv,' said Bugsy, when they were outside, 'was the most unconvincing performance from a bloke with some-thing to hide that I've ever heard, and I've heard plenty in my time. I didn't believe a word of it.'

'Neither did I,' agreed Jack.

CHAPTER TEN

Jack decided it was time for a WAWA meeting — Where Are We At. He called such meetings when a good deal of diverse information had been obtained by different officers. It was necessary to pull it all together to ensure everybody was singing from the same hymn sheet, although Jack hated that metaphor. For a start, he couldn't picture Bugsy singing from anybody's hymn sheet and if he did, he'd make up his own words. The idea of a WAWA was to prevent inquiries going off at a tangent and wasting resources through duplication and more often than not, it worked. Everyone was invited to contribute what they knew.

Standing in front of the whiteboard, Aled had written headings — WHO on one side and MOTIVE on the other. From his own interview, he wrote *Lady Helena* then for motive, 'financial gain' and 'freedom to have it off with Dickie N-S'.

'Couldn't she have done that anyway without doing away with Hugo?' asked Gemma.

'Good point, Gem, but I think she reckoned she'd get a better deal if he was dead and she was a baron's widow than if she had to slug it out with him in the courts and end up a disreputable divorcée,' explained Aled. 'And bear in mind that she's the mother of Rupert, the next Baron Fitzwarren, which must put her in a good position for any future financial support.'

'Would she have been physically able to do it?' asked Chippy. He was still young enough to see ladies as delicate flowers, despite his mother, a Professor of Music back home in New Zealand, being a feisty lady with no reservations about the power of women in modern society.

'Helena is very fit and stronger than your average woman in her forties.' Aled still had her finger-marks on his biceps from when she gave him a squeeze as he got up to leave the boat. 'All she had to do was persuade him to go down to the boathouse on some pretext where she'd already left the mace and helmet, then clout him over the head, shove on the helmet and splash! It's goodbye Lord Hugo — hello big payout.'

Gemma and Velma took over. Gemma wrote LOUISE under WHO. 'This lady had ample motive for wanting Hugo dead. He, and his frightful son, treated her like a brood mare bought at a prize livestock show to breed with their thoroughbred stallion. Unfortunately, the stallion, Rupert, wasn't fussy which fillies he mounted and the subsequent disease he picked up and passed on rendered poor Louise incapable of producing the heir that Hugo wanted, nor any other child, come to that.'

'You mean Rupert gave her a dose of the clap?' said Bugsy, just so that there was no misunderstanding.

'Yes, Sarge, you could say that.' Although Gemma had been trying hard not to, seeing it as demeaning and totally undeserved. 'Obviously, in that state, she'd no longer be any use to His Lordship and had he lived, he would have traded her in for a more fertile filly to mate with his son, not realizing it would have been the same childless result after he passed on the unpleasant disease. When Louise told him, he deeply resented such shocking claims against Rupert and accused her of having caught the disease from a lover but kept quiet about it for an easy life of wealth and privilege.' Gemma wrote that as the MOTIVE.

'Had I been Louise, I should have considered that more than a motive for murder and I'd have finished the job by taking one of those medieval daggers and turning his noble stallion son into a gelding.' Velma received a round of applause from all the female colleagues in the room including the canteen lady who'd only come up to deliver Bugsy's doughnuts.

'If she'd killed Hugo then fled to Scotland, wouldn't she have stayed there?' asked Jack. 'Surely the further away from Fitzwarren Hall the better.'

'I don't think so.' Velma frowned. 'She would have wanted to witness the destruction and scandal she had inflicted on the family at first hand. Watch them all suffer as she was suffering. But if you're asking me if I think she did it, sir, then the answer's no. Lord Hugo's death was premeditated and carefully planned, probably sometime in advance and based on long-held festering hatred. If Louise had done it, she would have been more likely to lash out spontaneously in her anger and frustration.'

'Are we putting Napier-Smarmy-Smythe on the board, guv?' Bugsy reckoned any bloke with his attitude and a predilection for spotty bow ties had to be up to something dodgy, even if they hadn't been able to prove it yet.

'Definitely.' Jack wrote his name under WHO. 'As Clive discovered, the investment company was losing huge sums of money from clients' accounts. We aren't yet able to identify whose offshore banks the money was being transferred to, although Fraud are on the case. There is every chance that it will turn out to be Lord Hugo, who Clive says isn't as wealthy as he led people to believe. However, if it is Napier-Smythe and Lord Hugo found out and threatened to shop him, that's a very good motive for shutting him up.' Jack wrote it under MOTIVE.

'And he's giving Lady Helena a regular seeing-to,' Bugsy chipped in.

'Not quite how I would have put it, Sergeant, but we get the drift.' Jack threw it open to the floor. 'Anyone else?'

'Lord Hugo's two children aren't up there,' said Aled. 'Do we think Rupert or Charlie might have wanted their father dead?'

'Not Charlie,' said Jack. 'She was very worried when Hugo went missing.'

'Yes, sir, but if you recall when we were speaking to Charlie on the farm, there was some friction when she wanted to move in with her partner, Danielle,' Gemma recalled. 'Lord Hugo seemed to think such a move would reflect badly on the Fitzwarren honour.'

'What pompous nonsense!' said someone at the back. 'The man was a dinosaur.'

'I agree,' said Jack. 'I believe I said something similar at the time. But do you think she would have gone as far as killing him?'

'Probably not, but the theatre of the armour, mace and helmet would have appealed to her,' Gemma decided.

'That leaves Rupert. Does anyone even know where he is?' asked Jack.

'Well, Louise doesn't. She intends only to contact him through her solicitor and after what he has done to her, she'll be going for the financial *vena jugularis*,' said Gemma. 'I was only thinking yesterday, the Fitzwarren motto, *Nemini Confidite* — *Trust No One* that I initially thought was weird has turned out to be totally appropriate.'

'I'm pretty sure Jamie Mackintosh knows more than he's letting on,' said Bugsy, writing up his name. 'Any luck getting into the database, Clive?'

'Not yet, Sarge, it's pretty tightly encrypted. But my team and I are still working on it.'

'What about the staff, sir?' Chippy was making copious notes on his computer. 'The maid Lord Hugo dismissed for stealing who turned out to be innocent. She must have held a grudge.'

'Louise said that was a year ago,' recalled Gemma. 'Would you wait that long before doing anything about it?'

'Revenge is a dish best served cold,' quoted Aled.

'Not that cold,' said Gemma. 'And how would she have got back into the house?'

'Maybe she had help from one of the staff. Mr or Mrs Beach might have let her in.' Chippy wrote MAID under possible suspects and SACKED under motive.

'Chippy has a point,' agreed Jack. 'We've been concentrating on members of the family without much success. Maybe we should take a closer look at the people who work there. We may have missed something important. Get over to Fitzwarren Hall and interview the prominent ones again. Well, that's it, folks.' He closed the meeting. 'We may have more questions than answers but I feel a breakthrough is imminent.'

* * *

It seemed sensible to start with the full-time staff who had been there the longest and had the closest connection to Lord Hugo and the Fitzwarren household. When Chippy approached her for help, Jessie Beach suggested Ted Greenslade, the head gardener.

'What Ted doesn't know about gardening you could write on a bay leaf, though you'd never guess it to look at him. With those big hands, it's hard to believe he has the dexterity for pricking out. He's been managing the gardens at Fitzwarren Hall longer than most of us can remember. I'd start with him, if I were you.'

Chippy found Ted in one of the greenhouses. He was sitting on an orange box, thumbing through a seed catalogue and dreaming of early flowering phlox. He looked to Chippy as if he was old enough to have been tending the extensive gardens of Fitzwarren Hall while the owner was away at the Battle of Hastings, but anyone over the age of forty looked ancient to Chippy.

'Good morning, Mr Greenslade.' He held out a hand which Ted shook with such vigour, Chippy was sure he could feel his fillings loosen. 'I'm Detective Constable Chippendale of the Metropolitan Police. We're investigating the death of Lord Hugo. I wonder if I might ask you some questions, please.'

Ted pulled out another orange box and motioned Chippy to sit. 'Right, officer, what d'you want to know?'

'How long have you worked here?' Chippy opened his note book.

'Erm . . .' Ted appeared to be counting on his fingers, '. . . forty years come Candlemas, and my old dad afore me.'

'Right,' Chippy was confused. 'So you knew Lord Hugo pretty well?'

'That I did, from when he was a nipper, and his old dad afore him. Mind, the least said about Baron William Fitzwarren the better.'

'Why is that?' Chippy was writing rapidly. This could turn out to be important background information.

Ted leaned forward and spoke conspiratorially. 'He had a terrible temper on him, especially when he was . . .' Ted made a wobbly motion with his hand imitating drinking from a glass.

'Do you mean Lord William was a drunk?'

'Shh!' Ted looked furtively to the right and left and put a finger to his lips. 'Dowager Beatrice never liked anyone to use that word. She said Lord William was highly-strung and the two bottles of brandy a day were medicinal, to relax him. It did that all right. Many's the time I found him stretched out on a pile of sacks in the potting shed, relaxed as a newt.'

Chippy processed this information, wondering if it had any connection to Baron William's subsequent demise on the motorboat although he'd read that the inquest report on the fatal accident concluded that it was the chauffeur, Sid Barnes, who was drunk at the tiller. 'What about Lord Hugo? Do you know of anyone with a grudge — anyone who might have wanted him dead?'

Ted took off his glasses, the lenses scarred from years of incautious pruning, and thought for a while, his head resting on his chest. Chippy thought he might have fallen asleep, then suddenly he said, 'No, can't say I do. Young Hugo was always very proud of the Fitzwarren name. Doubt if he'd have done anything to disgrace it and even if he had, it would have been kept very quiet. This family's good at hushing things up.'

'Such as what?' Chippy asked, eagerly.

'Dunno, do I? Like I said, they're good at hushing things up. Now, if there's nothing else, I've got a pond full of blanket-weed to sort out and I'm still having trouble with thrips.'

'Well, thank you, Mr Greenslade. You've been very frank.'

Ted sighed. 'You see the world for what it is after forty years in compost, son. People wouldn't have all these modern anxiety problems if they rolled up their sleeves and did a bit of mulching now and then.'

* * *

DC Dinkley was wandering about in the extensive Fitzwarren garages, looking for Carson, the chauffeur. Although he'd only been in post for a year and was the most recent member of staff to join the Fitzwarren household, he'd had daily contact with Lord Hugo which made him a person of interest. According to Bob Beach, Carson came with excellent references. He had filled the vacancy created when the previous incumbent retired. The role of chauffeur carried something of a covert health warning since the accident in the motorboat that had killed both Sid Barnes and Lord William. Even though it was fifteen years ago, it had been a hot topic of conversation at the time with all manner of conspiracy theories going the rounds and people had long memories. For that reason, it had been some time before a new chauffeur could be found and he had retired a year ago, creating the vacancy that Carson had filled.

Velma was admiring the splendid array of cars from the gleaming Bentley to the sleek E-type Jaguar when a voice behind her said, 'Can I help you, miss?'

Startled, she turned to find a handsome young man she judged to be about twenty-five, wearing a smart, dove-grey chauffeur's livery.

'Oh. Hello. You must be Mr Carson.'

'That's right, miss — George Carson. What can I do for you?' He was intrigued by the informal baggy sweater, jeans and square glasses.

Velma took out her ID. 'I'm Detective Constable Dinkley. You'll be aware that the Metropolitan Police are investigating the death of Lord Hugo Fitzwarren. I realize you've been interviewed already but I'd like to ask you a few more questions, if I may.'

'Yes, of course. Anything I can do to help. Everyone in the household is shocked. I understand that Lady Beatrice found His Lordship's body, then had a heart attack. I hope she's going to be OK. Apparently, she told her housekeeper he'd had an accident, but I don't know any more than that, as I told the last officer who questioned me.'

'For a number of reasons, the police are treating his death as murder.' Velma watched for a reaction, but his deadpan expression didn't change. 'How well did you know Lord Hugo?'

He answered without hesitation. 'Very well. I'd been his chauffeur for over a year, and I often drove him to his office in the city by motorboat. It was sometimes quicker because of the traffic. That was one of the reasons I got the job — I have licences to drive on the road and on the river.'

'Can you think of any reason why someone would want him dead?'

Again, his reply was immediate. 'Absolutely not. He was a good boss. Never unreasonable, always polite and he paid well.'

'So he didn't have any enemies that you can think of?'

Carson frowned. 'How do you mean, enemies?'

'Well, someone with a grudge or a score to settle.'

'I guess they've told you about Maggie, the maid who was sacked for stealing money from his desk.'

Velma wasn't surprised that he knew. She guessed rumours spread rapidly below stairs. She wondered if he knew that the

96

accusations had been false, but she wasn't about to explain. She was here to obtain information, not provide it. 'Have you seen Maggie at Fitzwarren Hall since?'

'No.' He paused, trying to remember. 'I believe she went to work in a cake shop in Richington Lacey.'

'Mr Carson, when was the last time you saw Lord Hugo alive?' Again, Velma watched his face for any hint of hesitation. There wasn't one.

'That would have been the night before he went missing. I drove him back from his office around eight o'clock, he thanked me like he always did, then he went inside the house, and I never saw him again.'

'And how did he seem — in himself?' It was an open question which required a personal opinion, but they were often the ones that provided the best clues.

He gave it some thought which Velma thought was reasonable because it was a while ago now. 'From what I remember, he seemed tired and a bit distracted — but then, he had been working late.'

'And when he went missing, didn't you wonder where he'd gone?'

'I'm not paid to wonder, miss, I'm paid to look after the cars and boats. I assumed His Lordship had gone away on business and would let me know when he returned and needed transport.'

Mentally, Velma put George Carson in the category of neurotypical but difficult to read. Neither of those definitions made him a killer. She thanked him for his time and left.

CHAPTER ELEVEN

Below stairs, in the very bowels of Fitzwarren Hall, Gemma was in the scullery sipping coffee and waiting for Winnie Arbuthnot to show up. Winnie washed the personal items of the family's clothing that were considered too delicate or expensive to be sent away to the laundry. She had been doing it for many years, so she was a staff member worth interviewing for her views on the deceased Lord Hugo. After waiting half an hour, Gemma had just decided that she would come back later, when there was a deafening clatter outside like someone falling downstairs with a hod full of bricks, followed by hoarse female cursing.

'Bloody hell! That's the third time today!' The door flew open and a plump lady with flushed cheeks staggered in, pushing a heavy-duty laundry trolley with two of the wheels hanging off. She wore a floral pinny over a pair of denim dungarees and flip-flops.

Gemma jumped forward to help her. 'Mrs Arbuthnot?'

The woman brushed away a strand of damp hair that had escaped from beneath the scarf tied around her head. 'That's right, dear. The younger members of staff call me Winnie the Pinny.'

Gemma consulted her notes. 'You're employed here as a laundress?'

'Actually, I'm a Garment Cleansing Operative. Who are you, dear?'

Gemma went through the routine of identifying herself. 'I was hoping you might be able to answer a few questions.'

'Well, if it's about laundry, you've come to the right place. Don't get one of these for a start.' She indicated the trolley, now lying on its side with washing spilling out of it. 'The advert said it was collapsible but it didn't say it collapses on its own when you're half-way down the stairs.'

'Oh . . . er . . . actually, I don't need a trolley. I have an Artificially Intelligent washer and a heat pump tumble dryer. They're in my kitchen so I don't have to carry my washing far.' Afterwards, Gemma wondered how she'd ended up discussing her laundry logistics when she'd come to talk about the murder of Lord Hugo, but it sometimes helped to gain a person's trust if you established some common ground.

'I see.' Winnie crossed her arms. 'And your knickers are always damp and smelly — am I right?'

'Er . . . well . . .' Gemma was lost for words.

'You know why, don't you? You don't peg out enough,' insisted Winnie. 'Modern laundry technology's fine if you don't mind your tights with the legs knotted and biological enzymes rotting your gussets. I can remember when knickers lasted. You wore them for ten years then cut them down for dusters. A triangle of lace with a thong up your bottom doesn't last five minutes, never mind the hygiene implications.'

'Yes . . . er . . . thanks for that. I'll remember to peg out more often.' Gemma needed to get Winnie back to the reason she was there. 'But do you think we could talk about Lord Hugo Fitzwarren?'

'If you like, dear, but he's dead. The old Dowager found him — well, what was left of him — floating in the boat-house. She keeps telling everyone that he had a tragic accident but I don't believe a word of it.'

'Really?' *Now we're getting somewhere more important than knickers*, thought Gemma. 'What do you think happened, Mrs Arbuthnot?'

'I don't think — I know. Someone bumped him off. And I'm not surprised.'

'Why do you say that?' Gemma wondered if she should have set her phone to record as the next few minutes could be vital evidence.

'Because he deserved it, that's why. He was a self-serving, bad-tempered, mean-minded arse, like his father before him. That woman isn't much better, either. They'd have been more suited living on Fitzwarren Farm.'

By 'that woman', Gemma assumed she meant Lady Helena. 'Why on the farm?'

'Because he was a pig and she's a cow. Between the two of them, they drove poor little Maggie into a breakdown. Accused her of stealing but it was all lies.'

'Do you mean Maggie who used to be a maid here?' Gemma remembered Lady Louise telling her about the incident but she hadn't mentioned a name.

'That's right. She's my sister's youngest. Honest as the day is long — she'd never have stolen money. Turned out Lady Helena admitted to taking it but they still sacked Maggie with no reference, no apology, nothing.'

With a background in law, Gemma asked, 'Why didn't she take them to an Industrial Tribunal for unfair dismissal and even defamation of character, if they branded her a thief? She could have claimed compensation.'

'You don't know Maggie. She's sensitive, vulnerable. She developed one of those eating disorders and started harming herself, poor little thing. Going to a tribunal would have terrified her — she'd never have coped.'

'That's awful. It should never have happened.' Gemma thought it might well have given someone a motive for killing Lord Hugo.

'Maggie's all right now, though,' continued Winnie. 'She got a job in her cousin's cake shop in Richington Lacey. It's where she was born and brought up. Her cup-cakes are the talk of the village.'

'Good. I'm glad. But you carried on working here, despite what happened to your niece?' Gemma thought she might have stayed, waiting for an opportunity for revenge. She was buxom with strong, muscular arms so could easily have been powerful enough to dispatch Lord Hugo.

'Too right I did. I charge a top hourly-rate and I get as much overtime and perks out of the miserable, lying skin-flints as I can.'

* * *

Jack sent Aled to speak to Maggie, telling him to take it gently. While he didn't have any serious suspicions after what Gemma had found out, it was a case of covering every angle and leaving nothing to chance. She could have had a burly brother who decided to get even on her behalf.

Aled drove to Richington Lacey and cruised along the only main street, looking for a cake shop. He parked outside, waited until it was empty, then went in and bought some cup-cakes. 'Hello. Nice day. Are you Maggie?'

She handed over his change and gave him a shy smile. 'Yes.'

Aled took out his ID, showed it to her and smiled back. 'They say your cup-cakes are the best,' he began, carefully. She looked thin and hollow-eyed. He guessed it was the aftermath of the eating disorder and felt guilty about reminding her of the circumstances that caused it, but that was what he'd come about, not just to stuff his face with cake. 'Are you enjoying this job better than the one you had at Fitzwarren Hall?'

She nodded. 'Oh yes. It was awful there. They said I'd stolen money.'

'Yes, but it wasn't true, was it? We know that. Have you been back since? Maybe to see your Auntie Winnie?'

She frowned. 'No, I haven't. I wouldn't set foot in that place ever again, no matter what wages they offered me.'

He paused while he swallowed a mouthful of cup-cake. 'Lord Hugo has been murdered. How do you feel about that?'

She thought about it for a bit. 'If you're asking if I'm sorry that he's dead? No, not really. But did I have anything to do with it? No, I didn't — definitely not.'

She was so obviously telling the truth that Aled saw no reason to question her further. 'Thanks for talking to me, Maggie. Your cup-cakes are the real deal.'

'You're welcome, officer. Enjoy the rest of your day.' She smiled and Aled left, relieved that he hadn't upset her.

When he got back to the nick, he updated the white-board which now had a long list of possible suspects and motives, both family members and staff, but nothing at all conclusive regarding the identity of the murderer. And they still hadn't found the Honourable Rupert Fitzwarren.

* * *

It was nine o'clock on a Friday night and Jack and Bugsy were still in the office. Garwood had been on the warpath, having overcome his dysentery-like disorder sufficiently to remain in the incident room longer than two minutes at a time. He had harangued Jack, accusing him of dragging his feet, although Garwood knew that wasn't really the case. However, the lack of a speedy result enabled him to fend off the Commander's irritating questions as to why he hadn't yet put DI Dawes forward for promotion to DCI because, in the Commander's own words, 'he was, quite clearly, the driving force behind the successes of the MIT and it was time for him to move on'. Garwood knew that promotion would mean losing Jack to another division — and probably his nucleus of top per-forming officers as well. They were fiercely loyal and would undoubtedly follow him. Inevitably, the clear-up statistics of what remained of Garwood's division would drop dramatically into the must-improve category. He couldn't let that happen, not if he was to retire with a knighthood as he planned. It went without saying that while he had Jack, he could claim to head up one of the most successful murder investigation teams in the Met. No, he couldn't lose Dawes, no matter what.

Jack and Bugsy were testing to destruction the information that the MIT had obtained over the last weeks — all the background checks, the alibis, the motives and the suspects. It was undeniably thorough, with every lead followed up, but still there was no breakthrough. Forensics couldn't help much more because of the state of the body and the contaminated crime scene. Opinions on the character of the deceased varied hugely but as Bugsy had pointed out, if you scratched the surface of any organization, you'd find some employees who thought the boss was great and some who thought he was a bastard, depending on their personal experiences. It was the same with families.

'Guv, what d'you reckon will happen to Fitzwarren Hall and the remaining members of the family if the Serious Fraud lads find out that Lord High-and-Mighty Hugo had been maintaining it from stolen money?'

Jack took off his glasses and pinched the bridge of his nose. 'Your guess is as good as mine, Bugsy. They can't arrest him now, obviously, but as far as Clive could establish, most of the missing money has been stashed away abroad in unidentifiable offshore accounts.' He passed a weary hand across his brow. 'It would be really helpful if we knew exactly what Lord Hugo's financial position was when he died. Whether he had mortgages or other debts, but only his solicitor will have that kind of information and he's keeping everything well hidden, regardless of warrants. There may not be any disposable income left at all.'

'So that would leave the family without any revenue. They might have to give up being economically inactive and sign on the dole or whatever it's called these days. That'll be a shock to their entitled systems.'

* * *

Jack was very late home, even for him. Corrie could tell he'd had a rough day from the way he plodded into the kitchen and kissed her on the cheek without saying anything. She didn't ask questions, just poured him a glass of wine and put his favourite supper in front of him — corned beef hash with baked beans and brown sauce. The sauce even came out of a bottle, of which she strongly disapproved. It wasn't that she was conforming to the dated stereotype of the little woman, pandering to the whims of the breadwinner by having his meal on the table the minute he walked in the door. As she pointed out on several occasions, if he had been a chef and she had been a copper, it would have been quite the other way around. But as it stood, the state of affairs suited them both.

She waited until he'd scoffed several forkfuls, then asked, 'Tough day?'

'Yes. Everyone is pulling their weight and we've examined every element of this case, several times over, but we don't seem to be getting any further forward. I don't suppose you've heard anything useful on your catering grapevine?'

'Funny you should ask. Cyn's Ladies Luncheon Club is running a book on who killed Hugo. As of yesterday, Helena is odds-on favourite. Louisa is close behind at three-to-one, and Rupert is down the field at fifteen-to-two. Beach the butler isn't in the running because they all like him and he's regarded as something of a hero for having resuscitated the old Dowager.'

Jack shook his head. 'Honestly, Corrie, I don't think running a book on a murderer is appropriate.'

'No, probably not. It certainly isn't evidence based but you know what Cyn's ladies are like.'

'I'm surprised Garwood hasn't put a stop to it.'

'He won't do that. He's got a tenner on Dickie Napier-Smythe.' She refilled his glass of Rioja. 'The editor of the *Echo* isn't much better. Apart from criticizing George Garwood, which is par for the course—' she giggled — 'Did you see what I did there? The golfing analogy?'

'Yes, the apocryphal game with the editor when George is supposed to have cheated.'

'Well, apart from that, the editor is sticking by his original unsubstantiated verdict that the deed was done by a random Trotskyist. He claims that there's a growing faction of militants in Kings Richington planning to overthrow the ruling classes and the police are doing nothing to stop them.'

'That's rubbish.'

'Yes, I know but it sells papers and gets him on social media.' She refilled her own glass of New Zealand Sauvignon Blanc and sipped it, appreciatively. 'I've been thinking about the Dowager's birthday ball and the vandalism to Baron William Fitzwarren's portrait. If the perpetrator was making a political statement against the aristocracy, I wonder why he wrote 'KILLER' on it. Why not 'FASCIST' or 'UP THE REVOLUTION?'

'Good point. The two events must be connected or it's too much of a coincidence.'

'And you don't believe in coincidences.'

'Correct. Is there any pudding?'

Corrie was about to say no, because Jack had already eaten double his quota of carbs for the day when the back door opened and Carlene appeared. She was carrying a food container which she opened and lifted out a Tarte Tatin.

'Hi folks. We had some dessert left after we closed and I thought you might like it. It just needs a scoop of ice cream.' She kissed them both and gave them a hug.

'Busy night, love?' asked Corrie, getting plates.

'Yep. It always is this time of year. Nobody wants a cold salad for dinner and fortunately for us, they'd rather come into the bistro than cook for themselves.' She sat down at the table. 'There was a lot of talk in the restaurant tonight about the Fitzwarren murder, Mr Jack. Are you any closer to catching who did it?'

Carlene had called Jack and Corrie 'Mr Jack and Mrs D' out of respect when she first moved into the flat they had provided for her at the age of sixteen, after she came out of local authority care. The titles had stuck and now it wouldn't have seemed right to call them 'Jack and Corrie'.

'What's the word on the street?' asked Jack. It never hurt to listen to *vox populi* and at the moment he needed all the help he could get.

'Well, the general view is that he was a pretentious little snob who deserved everything he got. As one lady put it, "he was so far up himself, he could have cleaned his teeth from the inside". As for who killed him, everyone seems to have a different opinion. There's a growing consensus that it was Lady Helena.'

'Why?'

'Because she'd found out about his affair with Céline.'

That made Jack sit up. He dropped his spoon. 'Who the hell is Céline?' His team had been working on this case for weeks with endless interviews and background checks and this was the first time he'd heard of any affair with a person called Céline.

'She's his personal assistant. French, apparently, and very attractive — much younger than him. Half his age, in fact.'

'How on earth do you get hold of this kind of information?' Jack was astounded.

'Well, you know what it's like in a busy restaurant, Mr Jack. I move about among the tables and I'm invisible. People say things while I'm serving without even realizing I'm there.'

'Do you know anything else about this Céline person?' Jack determined to get the troops onto it first thing on Monday morning.

'Only that she's the niece of a French lady related to Antoine's aunt who lives in Normandy. The woman who was telling her friend about it in the bistro works as a cleaner in Le Canard Bleu. She ate her way right through my set menu, twice, then I heard her mention that Lord Hugo had intended to marry Céline, if he hadn't carked it first.'

After Carlene had gone, Jack was deep in thought, trying to get some sense from this new information. When Corrie brought him a mug of coffee, he asked, 'Have you heard anything about Lord Hugo's affair with a girl called Céline?'

Corrie was cagey. 'Well, Cynthia may have said some-thing about it in passing.'

'So why didn't you tell me?'

'Because you're always saying I shouldn't listen to gos-sip and it's mostly fabricated by people with an 'angle' or a conspiracy theory.'

'Well, in future, if I say anything daft like that, ignore me.'

'Yes, dear.'

CHAPTER TWELVE

It was Saturday night and as usual, the city was rammed. The West End was pulsating with partygoers and socialites seeking the iconic nightlife that the cocktail bars, clubs, pubs and theatres provided. The lights were dazzling and the atmosphere was vibrant. Despite the cold, young ladies in crop tops, short skirts and sky-high heels went arm in arm with guys in fitted trousers, button-down shirts and jackets. It was a city full of lively people intent on having a good time.

A food delivery driver on a motorcycle emerged from a side street and filtered into the slow-moving traffic. Such drivers were a familiar sight on cold, dark nights when people wanted hot food but didn't want to face the elements to go out and fetch it themselves. The driver cruised down the road until he reached the Fitz Gallery where he stopped in the parking space outside and stood the bike up on its stand. Wearing jeans, a full-face helmet and a jacket bearing the logo of the takeaway, he attracted little attention from the throng of clubbers, queueing to get into the nightclub next door.

He took a pizza box and a plastic drinks bottle from the insulated delivery container on the back of the bike, smiling wryly at the warning on the bag — Caution Hot Contents. Strolling to the doors of the gallery, he looked up to confirm that the lights were on in the flat above. After a quick glance to his left and right, he poured the contents of the bottle through the letterbox. Inside the pizza box was a soaked rag which he lit with a match and pushed through on top of the petrol, shielding the operation with his body. He saw a gratifying flash of flame through the glass panels of the door, followed by a whooshing sound as the fire took hold. Satisfied with his work, he picked his way through the crowd that had spilled out into the road, climbed back on the bike and roared away.

By definition, an art gallery containing paintings in wooden frames, and such flammables as linseed oil and white spirit are an obvious fire risk if they aren't properly stored. Due to general disinterest and idleness on the part of the owner, the Fitz Gallery was a mass of flames in seconds. By the time the Fire Service arrived, a crowd had gathered. Someone pointed up at the roof and shouted, 'there are lights on in the top flat'. The fire fighters sprang into action and minutes later, two bodies were carried out, one in a body bag and the other on a stretcher, which was transferred to a waiting ambulance and whisked away to hospital.

* * *

The Metropolitan Police District, of which Kings Richington and the MIT were a part, consists of thirty-two London boroughs, but excludes the City of London — a largely non-residential and financial district, overseen by the City of London Police. DI Dawes started his career there as a constable, and he still had colleagues with whom he occasionally met up to watch a rugby match on the big screen in the pub, accompanied by a good deal of associated beverages. One of these colleagues had trawled the PNC — Police National Computer — for any information on the owner of the Fitz Gallery. He'd discovered that Jack had logged a professional interest, as it was connected to a murder case he was working on. Accordingly, he got in touch.

'Jack, how's it going out in the sticks?'

This was a standing joke, as Jack's promotion from Detective Sergeant to Detective Inspector in Kings Richington had been widely regarded by his city mates as a cushy move to rural obscurity where the only crimes were sheep rustling and fly-tipping. 'Real' crime never happened.

'Mike! Hey buddy!' Jack was at home, trying to fix the dishwasher, which Corrie said had developed a fault and was refusing to wash the dishes. 'It's Sunday. I thought you'd be shopping with your missus in the supermarket.'

'Nope. She has it delivered these days, and anyway there was an arson attack last night and I was called into the nick to deal with it. The reason I'm calling you is because the Fitz Gallery pretty much burned down late last night taking half of the nightclub next door with it. There's a tag on the PNC that you have an interest.'

That would have been put there by the ever-efficient Clive, thought Jack. 'Yes, it's part of an ongoing investigation into the murder of Lord Hugo Fitzwarren, 27th Baron of Richington.'

'Blimey, you've moved up the social ladder since you left the smoke,' quipped Mike. 'Bit of a change from the wannabe-Krays that you used to strong-arm into the cells.'

'That's right, and not so many drunks throwing up over your shoes. I'm guessing the gallery would have been empty at that time of night.' Jack had his fingers firmly crossed because the last information he had was that Rupert was staying at a club somewhere in the city and Lady Louise had gone back to her parents in Scotland.'

'Then you'd be wrong. The firefighters brought out two bodies from the living accommodation — a young man thought to be around mid-twenties who was taken to hospital suffering from smoke inhalation and a young woman of a similar age who was pronounced dead at the scene.'

'OK, Mike, thanks for the tip off. See you soon for a few jars.' Jack ended the call. He could see that Lord Rupert might have staggered back to the flat after a night of womanizing and heavy drinking. It would have been easier, given the traffic, than trying to make it home to Fitzwarren Hall, even if he'd phoned for the chauffeur to come and fetch him. But it was hard to believe that Lady Louise would have stayed there with him after what he had done to her and her firm assertion that she was going to divorce him and would only ever communicate via her solicitor.

While he was reflecting on how unfair life seems to be for some folk, Corrie appeared, carrying the instruction manual for the dishwasher.

'Haven't you fixed that yet? Honestly, Jack, you're a good copper but as a mechanic, you're about as much use as a one-legged man in an arse-kicking contest.'

'Rude,' said Jack. 'Are you sure it's developed a fault?'

'Well, it's either that or it's joined the National Union of Dishwashers and it's striking for shorter cycles.'

'Now you're just being silly. I've almost mended it but it's a very complicated piece of kit. It'll take at least another hour. Incidentally, I just got a call from Mike in the City Police. Someone burned down the Fitz Gallery last night and it looks like Rupert and Louise Fitzwarren were in the flat at the time.'

'Dear me, that's awful.' Corrie was dismayed. 'Are they OK?

'Not really. Rupert was taken to hospital with smoke inhalation but it seems Louise didn't make it. It's going to have an impact on the murder investigation, whichever way you look at it.'

'It'll have an even bigger impact on Louise's family.' She shook her head, sadly, trying to imagine how she would have felt if it had been Carlene in the bistro. It didn't bear thinking about. She turned her attention to the still silent dishwasher, then bent down, pushed a couple of buttons and pressed 'Start'. It burst into life and began making its usual swishing noises.

'Now, you see, I was just about to do that before you came in,' explained Jack. 'I'd already fixed it except for that last bit.'

'Of course you had, darling. How about you make us both a cup of tea? I don't think the kettle's on strike.'

* * *

Monday morning, Jack called a team meeting. They could tell from his face that something significant had happened over the weekend.

'Listen up, folks, this is important. On Saturday night, someone set fire to the Fitz Gallery.'

There were mutterings and a few sharp intakes of breath.

'It should have been empty but I'm sorry to say that it appears both Lord Rupert and Lady Louise were upstairs in the flat.'

'Are they all right, sir?' Both Gemma and Velma were concerned for Louise, having been the ones who had obtained the details of her appalling treatment by her husband.

'No, I'm afraid not. Lord Rupert is in hospital being treated for what appears to be lung damage from the smoke, and Lady Louise . . .' he hesitated, knowing both officers would be affected, '. . . I'm afraid she didn't make it. Obviously, no formal identification has been carried out yet.'

'Have we any idea who was responsible, guv?' asked Bugsy.

'I've had an update from a colleague in the City Police. The preliminary findings of the fire investigation officers report that the fire was caused by an accelerant, namely petrol, poured through the letter box and ignited, possibly with a rag. CCTV footage has identified a food delivery driver on a motorcycle pulling up outside, but because of the angle of the camera, which was positioned to capture footage of the nightclub next door, it wasn't clear what he had delivered. It looked like a pizza and a bottle of Coke. He returned to his bike and rode off. Unfortunately, the licence plate was obscured by a crowd of young people queueing to get into the club and because of how he was dressed, it could have been anybody.'

'So we don't have anything, sir?' Aled was blunt.

'Do we even know that it was the motorcycle delivery rider who torched the place?' wondered Bugsy.

'Not with any degree of confidence. He could have been exactly what he appeared to be.'

'Should we address the elephant in the room, sir?' asked Velma.

'You mean, is someone trying to wipe out the entire House of Fitzwarren?' Jack had been wondering the same thing ever since Sunday.

'Exactly. That's the 27th Baron murdered and an attempt on the life of the 28th Baron and his wife, all within a few weeks, to effectively ensure there'll never be a 29th, and we don't believe in coincidences, do we sir?'

'No, Velma, we don't. Obviously, the City Police are carrying out an investigation into the arson, as it took place on their patch, but we have a duty to notify Lady Helena of the injuries to her son and the parents of the late Lady Louise. But to avoid the potential for unnecessary distress, we need to wait until we have positive identification.'

'Given what we know about Rupert's proclivities, what if this delivery driver was the husband, boyfriend or father of one of the women he'd treated so badly?' Gemma asked. 'Somebody close who thought he should be prevented from doing it to anyone else.'

'It's a possibility,' replied Jack.

'Sir, I've been in touch with the pizza company whose logo was on this guy's jacket,' said Clive. 'They said they didn't make any deliveries to that part of the city on Saturday night, and apparently their jackets regularly get nicked.'

'So he was definitely bogus, but it was a good disguise,' conceded Jack. 'At that time of night, in a busy city, a food delivery driver could come and go without being noticed.'

'We don't have a clear picture on the CCTV footage. And afterwards, all but one of the cameras were destroyed by the fire,' reported Chippy. 'Can we even be sure it's a bloke? In that gear and helmet, it could just as easily be a woman. There must be plenty who'd like to see Rupert punished.'

'That's also a possibility,' agreed Jack, 'but I'm not sure fire would be their first choice of murder weapon.'

'Poor Louise,' said Velma. 'She may have led a privileged lifestyle for a while, but she paid the ultimate price for marrying a contemptible sleazeball like Rupert.'

While they were discussing these different scenarios, the phone on Jack's desk rang and Bugsy went across to answer it. When he came back, his expression was hard to define — somewhere between hope and disbelief. 'Guv, that was Norman. He says he has Lady Louise Fitzwarren on the desk. She's asking if it's all right with you if she goes back home to Scotland, now.'

This immediately generated a buzz of conversation, mainly questions about the real identity of the woman who was found dead in the torched flat. And much speculation, given that Chippy had raised the question of whether the arsonist could have been a woman, whether it had been Louise, seeking revenge.

Jack took Gemma down with him to speak to Louise, now in an interview room with a cup of tea. Jack began carefully. 'Since you're here Lady Louise, I wonder if you'd mind answering a few questions.' He indicated that Gemma should take over. 'You remember DC Fox?'

'Yes, of course,' she smiled at Gemma. 'But I'm plain Louise Fraser now. I've reverted to my maiden name and if I can go back home, I'm going to try to regain some of the happy life I had before I left. I've given instructions to my solicitor to go ahead with the divorce as quickly as possible and I hope I'll never have to set eyes on Rupert Fitzwarren ever again for as long as I live.'

Gemma took over. She wasn't sure how the news about Rupert fighting for breath in hospital would be received but she had a pretty good idea. 'Louise, there was an arson attack on the Fitz Gallery on Saturday night. Rupert was up in the flat. The firefighters got him out before the flames reached him, but he's in hospital suffering from the effects of smoke inhalation.'

There was a long moment of silence that you could have cut with a knife. Then Louise let out a spontaneous peal of laughter which she quickly stifled by putting her hand over her mouth. 'Oh dear. What must you think of me? Of course, there's nothing at all funny about this, but it's just that my first thought was inhaling smoke must have been a totally different experience to the substances Rupert normally inhaled on Saturday nights. Nothing at all like the cannabis he smoked or the cocaine that he snorted.'

'Louise, I have to ask this,' Gemma's tone was apologetic. 'Where were you on Saturday, say between the hours of ten and midnight?'

'That's OK, DC Fox. I can see this puts me right in the frame as suspect number one, but fortunately, I spent the whole night with a girlfriend in Kings Richington. We ate junk food, drank Prosecco and watched a film on Netflix. I've been there all weekend. It was a kind of celebration of my freedom from the Fitzwarrens. She'll be happy to confirm it. I'll give you her name and address.'

Gemma was relieved. She really hadn't wanted Louise to be questioned on suspicion of arson and attempted murder. She'd been through enough already. 'There was a young woman with Rupert. Would you know who she might be?'

'Not a clue. Some poor misguided girl that he picked up in one of the clubs. Did they get her out safely? Somebody should warn her that he's carrying a filthy disease and she'll need to be tested.'

'That won't be necessary,' intervened Jack. 'I'm afraid the young woman was pronounced dead at the scene.'

Louise looked sombre. 'Well, I'm very sorry about that. Whoever she was, she didn't deserve to die. She was taken in by his good looks and charm, as I was. It's a lesson I needed to learn but at least I survived the experience.' She stood up. 'Well, officers, am I free to go home to Scotland, once you've confirmed my alibi?'

'Yes, of course.' Realistically, Jack had also eliminated her from any involvement in the murder of Lord Hugo so he had no reason to keep her. 'Good luck, Louise.' They heard her thanking Sergeant Parsloe for the tea on her way out.

* * *

Back in the incident room, Aled asked, 'Has anyone else spotted the significance that sex has had on this family over the years?'

'I don't understand why sex is so important,' said Chippy.

'In that case, you're not doing it properly,' muttered someone and there was subdued sniggering from the people at the back, quickly quelled by a stern look from Bugsy.

'No, seriously,' Aled continued, 'there's Lord Rupert screwing anything with a pulse, his mother Helena doing much the same, Beatrice and her surgeon boyfriend who were probably at it behind old William's back while he was drunk and the late Lord Hugo whose entire *raison d'être* was to ensure there were heirs to continue the line.'

'Which is why he was so against Charlie and Dani's relationship. No new Lord Fitzwarrens were likely to result from that,' Chippy agreed.

'Reproduction is a risky business,' announced Gemma, vowing to avoid it at all costs.

'Swallows have the right idea,' mused Clive. 'They can do it at a combined velocity of sixty miles per hour. There's no time for online dating or intense discussions about who's treating whom as a sex object.'

'Yeah, and then they crap all over your garage roof and sod off back to Africa,' said Bugsy with feeling. 'Hardly the model for a long-term, loving relationship.'

'I think you've hit the nail on the head, Sarge,' said Velma. 'Long-term loving relationships aren't what's important to the Fitzwarrens — and that's what has caused all the trouble.'

It was much later when Jack realized that in the distraction of the arson attack on the Fitz Gallery, he'd forgotten all about 'Céline'.

CHAPTER THIRTEEN

With Sir Hugo dead and Charlie moved out to the farm, Lady Helena found herself rattling around in Fitzwarren Hall. Beatrice was in the Dower House, being fussed over by Monty and her housekeeper, and she had no idea where Rupert was. It really was too bad of him, staying away when he knew Mummy was on her own and miserable. She was even having trouble contacting Dickie. She'd been to his boat several times, looking for him, but it was deserted. He'd even taken away his belongings, and the marine administrator seemed to think the cabin cruiser was up for sale. Dickie wasn't at his flat in Kensington, either. The last time they spoke, it was to discuss how soon after the reading of Hugo's Will they could go away together. Dickie had been annoyingly reticent, saying they should wait, for the sake of appearances. Why were men so unreliable? It was while she was pouring yet another gin and tonic and pondering gloomily over her future, that Beach appeared.

'My lady, DI Dawes and DS Malone are here to see you. They have something important to discuss.'

She groaned. 'Not those two ghastly plods again. Tell them I can't see them, I have a sick headache.' She put the back of her hand to her brow in a theatrical gesture.

Beach felt the sickness had more to do with the half bottle of gin that had gone from the decanter he'd filled up that morning than a headache. 'I really think you should see them, my lady. It's about Lord Rupert.' Beach had a good idea what was coming. When Louise had been lonely and needed someone to confide in, she had become close to Jessie Beach during her time at the Hall. Before she left for Scotland, Louise had told Jessie about the fire and Rupert's anonymous girlfriend who had sadly succumbed to the smoke, so Bob prepared himself for the inevitable screaming fit when Her Ladyship found out.

'Oh, all right, if I must,' she grumbled, irritably. 'But come back and show them out after five minutes. Make some excuse. Say I've been called away to deal with an urgent matter and they have to leave.'

Jack and Bugsy entered the living room after Beach had announced them and showed her their ID as a courtesy, although Helena knew perfectly well who they were. She did not ask them to sit down but stayed where she was, reclining on the enormous sofa with a glass in her hand.

No barking spaniels, this time, so Jack guessed Charlie had taken them with her when she moved out to the farm. He started cautiously, not wanting to trigger a display of hysterics or a fainting fit. 'It's about your son, Lord Rupert, my lady.'

She gave an exaggerated sigh. 'Oh dear. What is it this time? Let me guess. One of your over-enthusiastic constables found a microscopic speck of weed in his pocket and wants a pat on the head for arresting him.'

Fed up with the snotty, entitled attitude of this load of snobs, Bugsy had no qualms about being blunt. He decided that if she had a hissy fit, he'd grab the nearby soda syphon and squirt her with it, and to hell with complaints to the IOPC. 'Your son is suffering from respiratory failure and he's in hospital on a mechanical ventilator.' He was gratified to see that this wiped the supercilious smirk off her face.

'What?' She jumped up and tottered slightly, either from the shock or the gin. 'No! It isn't true. You're just saying that to upset me.'

'Lady Helena, we have nothing to gain by upsetting you,' said Jack. 'We're just here to inform you that somebody set fire to the Fitz Gallery on Saturday night while your son was in the flat and he inhaled the smoke.'

Beach came in then, to show the officers out as she'd instructed. She'd obviously forgotten. 'Beach, not now! Something terrible has happened. Get Carson. I need him to drive me to the hospital immediately. Lord Rupert may be dying.' She also seemed to have forgotten about Jack and Bugsy and swept out, snivelling.

'May I show you out, officers?' Beach was his usual implacable self.

'Mr Beach, you probably know this household and its occupants better than anybody,' suggested Jack. 'Might you have any information about the recent goings-on that would be useful to us?'

'Sadly, no, sir. But I will let you know if anything comes to light.'

* * *

Back in his butler's pantry, Bob Beach was on the horns of a dilemma. He sat, deep in thought for some time, then he went to find Jessie. She had been discussing meals with the cook who wanted to know if there was a remote possibility that somebody, at some time in the foreseeable future, would require a meal, otherwise she was going home to feed her own family.

'Jess, do you think I should tell them — those two police officers?' Bob was still thinking about the question the senior one, DI Dawes, had asked as he was leaving. It was almost as if he knew that there was something he hadn't mentioned.

'Tell them what?' Jessie asked.

'About His Lordship's briefcase and the phone we found in the priest hole.'

She thought about it. 'It rather depends on whether you think they have any relevance to Lord Hugo's murder or the arson attack that nearly killed Mr Rupert — or Lord Rupert as he is now, I suppose.'

'Well, they must have, mustn't they? Otherwise, why would Lord Hugo have locked documents inside a briefcase and hidden them with his phone down a priest hole. I mean, hardly anyone knows it exists apart from us. It was only by chance that I spotted him going down there late one night. If they weren't significant, he'd have kept them in his desk with all his other papers.'

'Maybe we should hand them to Mr Mackintosh and let him decide,' suggested Jessie.

'Good thinking, love. I'll give them to George to drop off at Mackintosh's office tomorrow. He's at a bit of a loose end with only Lady Helena to drive about.'

* * *

Rupert's eyes were closed. The motor, moving air through the ventilation system, released vibrations and a steady mechanical throb. The consultant had told Helena that although His Lordship could neither move nor speak, his brain could still process sounds and sensations so he was able to hear and feel everything around him. If she continued to spend her time in his room panicking and weeping, it would unnerve her son and the hospital would have to ask her to leave. She should talk to him in a calm voice and hold his hand to help him feel at ease.

Helena looked at Rupert lying there helpless, his shock of wavy black hair against the white pillow — like a glossy raven's wing in the snow, she thought, fancifully. His olive, Mediterranean complexion, usually so tanned and attractive, seemed to have paled. It was little wonder, thought Helena, that silly young women threw themselves at him, he was so heartbreakingly handsome and reminded her of his father. She dismissed that thought almost before it had taken shape.

'Rupert, my darling boy.' She picked up his limp hand and kissed it. 'Mummy's here, now. You're going to be all right. As soon as you're well enough, we'll have you moved to the private hospital where they looked after Grannie. You don't belong here amongst these common people and rude doctors.'

She glanced at her phone — still no message from Dickie. She rang his number, desperate for his support but got voicemail for the twentieth time. Where could he possibly have gone without telling her and after all the plans they'd made to go away together?

* * *

Dickie Napier-Smythe was taking a shower after the eleven-hour flight from London Heathrow to Owen Roberts International Airport in the Cayman Islands. His house, just ten minutes from Camana Bay, had been a snip at just over three million dollars — only a fraction of the money he had deposited in banks there, over the last couple of years. That was the trick — little and often, so as not to attract attention, and only from those investments and funds where there was little movement, which usually meant the elderly and very rich clients. Dickie congratulated himself on being clever enough to steer the police towards the conclusion that it was Hugo who had been syphoning money away from the business. Poor old Hugo, he hadn't a clue. He was so busy trying to preserve his precious pedigree that he couldn't see what was going on right under his rather large nose. Dickie suspected that had been the case for years and not just about finance.

After his shower, Dickie went out onto the pool deck with a Cayman Jack Margarita. By now, his sudden and enduring disappearance must have indicated to Helena that their relationship was over — or maybe not. She had a great body but she was never what you might call quick on the uptake. There was a time when he thought she might have disposed of Hugo herself or persuaded someone else to do it, but after the subsequent arson attack, he changed his mind.

There was no way she would endanger the life of her beloved Rupert. There was obviously someone else who wanted to put an end to the Fitzwarren family. Well, good luck to them, thought Dickie. Nothing to do with him any longer. He smiled to himself, wondering how the Serious Fraud officers were getting on, auditing the company's severely compromised finances. Smugly, he believed he'd covered his tracks pretty well, although they'd probably get there in the end. But now he was out of reach with a new identity and it was too late. He was aware that the UK had an extradition treaty with the Cayman Islands, but for that to work, they first needed to know his name and where he was. He finished his drink, shrugged off his dressing gown and dived into the pool.

* * *

'Sir, I've traced the young woman who was in the Fitz Gallery with Rupert. She was Tracey Shuttleston, a cocktail waitress at the Purple Parrot,' announced Clive.

'I know it,' said Aled. 'It's one of those fancy clubs just off Mayfair. It's where the rich and beautiful people gather to break all the rules.'

'How come you know it?' demanded Gemma. 'You're not rich or beautiful.'

'How very unkind,' said Bugsy. 'The lad can't help it if he's poor and plain.'

'Thanks, Sarge — I think.' Aled frowned.

'The City Police have her details and have undertaken to notify her parents as part of their investigation into the arson and what they are presently treating as manslaughter,' added Clive. 'The Shuttlestons live somewhere in Lancashire.'

'If the Fitzwarrens had an ounce of decency, they'd offer to pay for the funeral,' said Gemma.

'I think they might find that a bit awkward at the moment.' Clive had been delving again. 'Before someone put a premature end to his baronial tour of duty, Lord Hugo was attempting to remortgage Fitzwarren Hall for the third time. As far as I can see, in every practical sense, he was broke.'

'That would explain why he was stealing from his finance company,' reckoned Bugsy.

'Sarge, I'm not sure that he was,' said Clive. 'I've had my team going through his finances with a fine toothcomb. If he was stashing the cash in offshore bank accounts ready to leg it, why try to remortgage the Hall? And he'd been borrowing from the bank to support Fitzwarren Farm, all the staff and the family members. His overdraft makes mine look almost miniscule. It doesn't make any sense.'

'Then it had to be Napier-Smythe,' concluded Jack. 'Let's pick him up. And while we're there, I think we should talk to Céline, the late Lord Hugo's personal assistant.'

'Did we know about her, sir?' asked Aled.

'No, we didn't. I only found out about her by chance, but she's definitely a person of interest. If the rumours are correct, she was earmarked to become the next Baroness Fitzwarren.'

* * *

The receptionist in the outer office of Fitzwarren & Napier-Smythe Asset Management declared that she hadn't seen Mr Napier-Smythe for over a week. 'When you find him,' she declared, more than a trifle miffed, 'would you please remind him that I haven't been paid for two months?'

'Did he ask you to make any travel arrangements for him when you last saw him?' asked Jack.

'No, he didn't. I've had Lady Helena on the phone all hours of the day and night, demanding that I tell her where he's gone. She seems to think I have him imprisoned in the stationery cupboard as a sex-slave. Some of the clients are getting restless, too. First Lord Hugo disappears then turns up dead and now they can't reach Mr Napier-Smythe. It isn't good for the reputation of the company, I don't mind telling you. I've already applied for another job — one where you actually get paid — so I shall be out of here very soon.'

'While we're here,' began Jack, 'do you think we could have a word with Céline? I believe she was Lord Hugo's personal assistant.'

The receptionist sniffed. 'I'm afraid not. She pushed off back to France as soon as she found out Lord Hugo was dead, leaving me to do everything.'

'Did she leave a forwarding address?'

'No, she didn't. I've no idea where she went and her surname was Dubois, so good luck with tracing her amongst all the others in France. Now, if you'll excuse me . . .'

They left her attempting to answer several phones which were all ringing at once.

* * *

'Looks like Napier-Smythe's done a runner, guv.' They were outside in the car eating fish and chips that Bugsy had fetched from a nearby chippy.

'And it's too late to put out a port alert.' Jack wondered what Corrie would say if she could see him devouring greasy battered cod and limp chips with his fingers, out of a polystyrene box, but both coppers had been ravenous, having had nothing to eat since breakfast. Bugsy claimed his brain didn't work properly when he was hungry. 'But I don't honestly see Napier-Smythe as a realistic suspect for Lord Hugo's murder, do you?'

'No, guv. I know we tried to put the wind up him about his relationship with Lord Hugo's wife and he got a bit shirty, but he wasn't dialled into her enough for it to be a motive for murder.'

'In that case, if he isn't a suspect in our murder and attempted murder cases, it's up to the Serious Fraud team to find him.'

'What about this Céline Dubois, guv? Is she sufficiently involved in the murder for us to try to find her?'

Jack wrinkled his brow. 'Dunno, yet. I think we need to know more about her and her relationship with Hugo than just the gossip that's going around the grapevine.'

CHAPTER FOURTEEN

Bob Beach found Carson in one of the garages, polishing the Bentley. 'Nice job, George. I can see my face in it.'

'Thanks, Mr Beach. It's not really the same now that I don't use it to drive Lord Hugo to his office. With Lady Beatrice still poorly, the only person who uses the car is Lady Helena. I'm guessing that means the family will have to let me go.'

'I hope not, George. But if they do, with your credentials, you should get another job easily. In the meantime, I wonder if you would do me a favour.' Bob held out the leather briefcase that he'd found in the priest hole. It had Hugo's initials and the Fitzwarren coat of arms printed in gold foil on the front. 'Could you drop this off to the solicitors, Mackintosh & Mackintosh? It needs to go to Jamie Mackintosh. I don't know what's in it, but obviously it's for the lawyers to sort out. And there's Lord Hugo's phone. I've sealed it up in this padded envelope. Tell them that the items were found in a secret location and that we can't be sure how long they'd been there.'

'Of course, Mr Beach. I'm glad to be of some use. I'll take one of the smaller cars as I'm not driving one of the family.'

* * *

The young lady behind the desk smiled. 'Good afternoon, sir. How can I help?' She took in at a glance the dove-grey uniform, the cap under his arm and the immaculate white gloves. Very smart. She guessed he hadn't come to consult one of the partners over a driving misdemeanour or a parking fine.

George handed over the locked briefcase and the envelope containing the phone. 'Good afternoon, miss. I'm George Carson, chauffeur to the Fitzwarren family. Could you please give these to Mr Jamie Mackintosh? They belonged to the late Lord Hugo Fitzwarren and have only recently come to light.'

'Yes, of course.' She bit her lip. 'What a terrible thing to happen. I met His Lordship a couple of times when he came here to see Mr Mackintosh. Such a gentleman and very charming.'

'Yes, he was. The best employer anyone could wish for. We all miss him very much.'

She lowered her voice. 'Are the police any closer to finding out who did it?'

'I couldn't say, miss. We've all been questioned but they don't give much away.'

'I'll take these straight in to Mr Mackintosh. Then, if you're not in too much of a hurry, I could make you a cup of tea before you go back out into the cold.'

'That would be very kind. Thank you.'

* * *

In his office next door, Jamie had just finished a phone conversation with a potential client wanting urgent legal advice. It seemed he was four months overdue with his rent, his wife had run off with a double-glazing salesman and the dog had just eaten his glasses. Jamie was a good lawyer but he couldn't work miracles. What this unfortunate man needed was a debt advisor, a relationship counsellor and a vet — not a lawyer. He decided to hand it over to one of the paralegals — it would be good experience for them.

Grateful for the distraction, he prised open the lock on Lord Hugo's briefcase using a letter knife, then extracted the papers. He read through them slowly, one page at a time, becoming increasingly astonished. Hugo had only hinted at this on Jamie's frequent visits to Fitzwarren Hall and the lawyer hadn't really believed it was true, but here it was, in black and white. Little wonder it was in hard copy — Hugo wouldn't have wanted it available online to be hacked by anyone with the skills. Among other staggering conclusions, he realized that it meant the list of suspects for Hugo's murder was considerably longer than he first thought. On the plus side, there was a good chance that nobody else had seen the papers. His next steps were far from clear. Finally, he decided he needed to consult his father, Angus, for advice, but not before he had worked out the practical and legal implications of Hugo's last instructions.

* * *

Angus Mackintosh was semi-retired and only came into the city if there was anything he was particularly interested in or when his son was unsure about some legal point and needed his advice. The Fitzwarren case came into both categories. His office hadn't changed since he had worked there full time — paintings of Highland cows and stags in the heather hung on the walls, and in his desk drawer, a bottle of Speyside Malt and a tin of shortbread, both forbidden by his doctor because of his rising blood sugar.

'Dad, have you had a chance to look at those papers yet?' Jamie had taken them into his father's office and put them in front of him personally rather than risk anyone else seeing them.

Angus sat back in his chair and took a deep breath. 'I've read them right through three times and I still can't believe it. You've been acting for the family for some years — did you get any hint of what Lord Hugo is claiming here?'

'Yes, but only a hint. I didn't realize the full implications. Of course, once it's put in front of you, you begin to see things that you didn't notice before and it starts to make sense.'

Angus frowned. 'All this is going to cause a great deal of upset, laddie, particularly the proposed new Will, despite the fact that he didn't get a chance to sign it. We need to be sure of our position here. I foresee a lot of accusations and apportioning of blame. We don't want complaints to the Law Society about how we handled it.'

'I agree. It also adds another motive to the possible suspects in Lord Hugo's murder.' Jamie was thinking he might have to share what he suspected with the police.

'You mean someone wanted to kill him before he got a chance to sign the Will?' said Angus. 'It wouldn't be the first time something like that had happened in a dysfunctional family.'

'It's a distinct possibility. I haven't been able to get into his phone — he had it protected with all kinds of safety systems and I don't want to ask one of those mobile phone chappies with a stall in the arcade who offer to unlock your phone for a tenner. It would be a huge breach of confidentiality. What do you think I should do next, Dad?'

Angus thought for a while. 'Give the phone to the police. They'll have someone who knows how to unlock it and decipher what's on it. And they're obliged to keep it confidential. Then speak discreetly to Lady Helena. After all, she's the one who will be most affected. But be prepared for fireworks. She isn't going to take this lying down.' He picked up one of the items. 'Have you seen one of these kits before?'

'Yes. You can download them off the internet. Several of my clients have used their services, then afterwards, they ended up consulting me about the results.'

Angus tutted. 'My goodness, how times have changed since I was practising. There was never anything like this. It would have stirred up all kinds of mischief that's best kept hidden.'

'That's exactly what it did. I'll make an appointment to see Lady Helena. Thanks for your advice, Dad.'

After he'd gone, Angus decided it would be prudent to speak to old Barnaby, next time he was in the club. Get the inside information on how the law would view all this — without giving anything away, naturally. He opened his drawer — to hell with it! He poured a generous shot of single malt and popped a piece of shortbread in his mouth.

* * *

Clive was triumphant having found what he had been looking for after many failed attempts — the coroner's report following the inquest into the deaths of Baron William Fitzwarren and Sid Barnes, some fifteen years ago. He knew that once an inquest had been completed, a properly interested person, such as himself, a digital forensic specialist in the Met, is allowed to inspect the evidence put forward at that inquest and a copy of the post-mortem examination report. For some reason, they had been purposely archived in such a way as to make them difficult to locate. The reason given was that every attempt had been made to avoid upset to the private lives of the people involved. To Clive, that sounded suspiciously like a cover up and only served to make him dig deeper.

'Sir, I've managed to unearth a copy of the coroner's report you asked for.'

'Good man, Clive.' Jack was grateful for any sign of progress. The longer this case went on, the more complications it seemed to throw up. 'Does it tell us anything useful?'

'I'm not sure, sir, but it makes interesting reading, if only because someone took great pains to make it difficult to find.'

'Forward it to me, Clive, and thanks.' Jack spent some time studying the report. By the end, he had a pretty good idea why it had been kept under wraps. The influence of the Fitzwarrens at that time had certainly been considerable. The coroner had returned an open verdict on both deaths, recording that there was insufficient evidence to decide how the deaths came about. The case was left open in the event that further evidence appeared. Which, of course, it hadn't.

'Listen up, team.' He went to the front of the room. 'What do we make of this?' He read it out. 'The activity in the motorboat leading up to the fatal accident was witnessed by certain bystanders on the bank and tourists in a passing pleasure boat on the Thames. They were unanimous in having seen the two occupants — that would have been Baron William Fitzwarren and the chauffeur, Sid Barnes fighting, just before the crash. One witness, a panel beater from Dagenham, said it was real vicious stuff with the big bloke, that would have been Fitzwarren, landing several hefty punches, while the little bloke, Barnes, tried to control the boat and defend himself at the same time. Eventually, the inevitable happened and the boat hit one of the Hammersmith Bridge supports and burst into flames. They found a petrol can amongst the wreckage indicating that the boat had been carrying extra fuel, causing an explosion and the subsequent inferno.'

'Blimey, that must have been nasty,' commented Bugsy. 'I wonder what they were fighting about.'

'According to what the Commander told me at Lady Beatrice's birthday party, the rumour was that the chauffeur had been drinking. Sir Barnaby said, and I quote, 'they were both burnt to a crisp so they couldn't prove anything for certain.'

'How very unpleasant,' said Gemma, wrinkling her nose.

'But interestingly, the post-mortem hinted that, on balance of probability, it was Baron Fitzwarren who was inebriated, although there wasn't much of him left to test.' Jack was writing the salient points on the board.

'I think that's the more likely scenario,' said Chippy. 'When I interviewed the head gardener, Ted Greenslade, he said the old baron got through two bottles of brandy a day and that he frequently found him pissed — sorry — passed out in the potting shed.'

'That's useful information, Chippy,' said Jack. 'I bet Lord Hugo was instrumental in making it look like the fault of the chauffeur.'

'The honour of the Fitzwarrens was at stake.' Aled was scornful.

'Never mind the adverse financial implications or embarrassing publicity,' said Bugsy.

'Do we think that's the dark family secret that the Dowager is so desperate to hide?' asked Gemma.

'No.' Velma was positive. 'It's bad enough but I believe it's something much worse. I don't think we're even close yet.'

'Did you get a crystal ball along with your psychology degree, Velma?' asked Bugsy.

She laughed. 'No, Sarge. But case studies and surveys indicate that people in general wouldn't consider a bibulous baron to be especially unusual or shocking. I bet there are loads of them sleeping it off in the House of Lords as we speak. But bashing your chauffeur is something else entirely — enormously infra dig amongst the gentry. I'd love to know what the fight was about.'

* * *

'Don't motorboats have a dead man's thingummy, like trains?' asked Corrie from under the kitchen sink. Following her success with the dishwasher, she was applying her newfound DIY skills to plumbing. The water had been taking ages to run away and she'd rightly guessed that there was some kind of blockage.

'Yes, they do.' Jack had been filling her in on the more interesting aspects of the coroner's report, while holding a bucket of the gunge and backed up water that had drained out when she unscrewed the u-bend. 'A dead man's switch is a sort of cord attached to the driver at one end and to a key mounted on the switch at the other.' He looked doubtfully at the pipes. 'How did you know what to do?'

'Because a nice young man on YouTube showed me. So did the Fitzwarren boat have a thingummy?'

'Dunno, it was too badly burned to tell. Of course, there have been occasions where some idiot who thinks he's smart fixes the cord to part of the boat instead of the operator,

131

just for convenience. The chauffeur might have done that. We'll never know.' He tried to peer at what she was doing. 'I suppose you did turn off the water, first? We don't want it flooding all over the floor.'

'Of course I did. What do you take me for?' She straightened up. 'I think that's cleared it. Now, I just need to . . .'

'Good,' said Jack. 'I can get rid of this. It smells.'

She grabbed his arm. 'No, don't do that!' But it was too late. Jack emptied the bucket of filthy gunge down the sink, where it went right through and flooded out onto the kitchen floor.

Corrie took a deep breath. 'As I was about to say, I just need to reconnect the u-bend.'

Jack looked sheepish. 'I'll fetch the mop and bucket, shall I?'

CHAPTER FIFTEEN

With her precious Rupert moved to a comfortable room in a private hospital, and now able to breathe on his own, Helena allowed herself some pamper time at her favourite health spa. She'd had her toxins purged, her mind and body relaxed and her chakras unblocked and now she felt ready to face the next ordeal — she was sure there would be one before this beastly run of unpleasantness was over.

She summoned Carson who drove her back to Fitzwarren Hall where Beach opened the vaulted, heavy oak front door.

She swept in, throwing her jacket and tote bag at him. 'Any messages for me, Beach?' She still hadn't heard from Dickie and feared he must have had some kind of accident. Why else wouldn't he have contacted her?

'Yes, my lady. There has been one.'

'Was it Mr Napier-Smythe?' She was filled with anticipation. 'Where is he? Did he leave a contact number? Quickly, tell me.' Soon Dickie would come to take her away with him, and now that Rupert was out of danger, she would go.

'No, my lady.' Beach's expression did not change although inside he was thinking *you silly woman*'. 'It was Mr Mackintosh. He wants to make an appointment to discuss something with you.'

'Oh, for goodness sake! Will they never leave me alone? First those frightful policemen and now the solicitor. I've only just been widowed — don't they understand I need privacy to grieve. Ring him back and tell him I'll let him know when I feel up to it.'

'Very well, my lady, as you wish. But he did mention that it was important, something to do with Lord Hugo's Will.'

Helena had already taken three steps up the staircase to her private sitting room. She came back down. 'Did he say what exactly?'

'Not to me, my lady.' *As if he would*, thought Beach. *I'm just the butler. But if I were a betting man, I'd put money on it being something he found in Lord Hugo's private briefcase or on his phone.*

'In that case, I suppose I'd better see him. Tell him I could spare ten minutes tomorrow morning at eleven.' She continued up to her room, needing gin and tonic and time to think.

* * *

That evening, the lounge of the St James's gentlemen's club was half empty. It was very cold outside and given that many of the members were in the autumn of their years, they had been reluctant to leave the warmth of their homes. Since Lady Lobelia was at her Zumba class, Sir Barnaby was in his usual leather armchair by the log fire. He had enjoyed an excellent fillet steak and chips and spotted dick and custard in the dining room and was reading the *Times* and drinking a rather fine cognac in the lounge.

'Och aye, Barnaby. How ye doing?' Angus Mackintosh appeared carrying a rapidly diminishing single malt.

'Scotty! Good to see you.' He motioned for him to sit in the Chesterfield armchair opposite. 'Haven't seen you since the Fitzwarren bash.'

'Trying to take it easy, these days. The quack keeps threatening me with high blood pressure, diabetes and a dozen other ailments that stop me enjoying myself.' He pointed to Sir Barnaby's brandy. 'Let me get you another one of those.' He gestured to the steward and ordered the drinks.

'So what brings you out on this frosty night?' Barnaby asked.

'To be honest, I was hoping to bump into you. Need some advice. It's to do with the Fitzwarrens but it's very hush-hush.' He put a finger alongside his nose.

The commander was curious. 'You're the legal expert — all those years in the Home Office. What do you need from me?'

'First, let me tell you about the information that has been put before Mackintosh & Mackintosh. Then I need you to tell me what the police position is, given that your chaps are conducting an investigation into Lord Hugo's murder.'

'OK Scotty. Fire away.'

Mackintosh outlined the situation for several minutes, after which Barnaby said, 'Bloody hell, Scotty! Are you sure about all this?'

'I'm as sure as I can be. I've seen the documents. Lord Hugo had them hidden in a priest hole.'

'I bet he did. Well, I always thought the Fitzwarrens were a rum lot but I didn't see that coming. What does your boy propose to do next?'

'I've advised Jamie to speak to Lady Helena since it mainly involves her. What would you advise, from the police angle?'

'I'd make sure he's wearing full riot gear and carrying a taser gun. Seriously though, Scotty, I think one of my officers should be present. There are several implications here, not least additional motives for someone to want Lord Hugo dead.'

'What if the woman refuses to have the police there at the meeting?' Mackintosh felt sure she would object.

'Then tell her she'll be arrested on suspicion, taken down the station in handcuffs and interviewed under caution. From what you say, she's already broken several laws and now she's very likely a person of interest in a murder case.' He waved to the steward. 'Shall we have another round? After all that, I think we've earned it.'

* * *

Under the same principle as the direction of rolling excrement — problems originating at the top of the chain of command tended to become the responsibility of those lower down — the job of sitting in on the interview was devolved from Sir Barnaby to DCS Garwood who finessed a finger-tip pass down to Jack.

'Dawes!' Garwood shouted to him across the incident room. 'The Commander wants you to accompany Mackintosh during his interview with Lady Helena. I've no idea what it's about but he says it's going to be tricky and he needs you to ride shotgun.'

Jack hoped that wasn't in the literal sense. He knew these toffs with country estates were pretty good shots. 'Right, sir. What am I looking for?'

'What we police officers are always looking for, evidence of wrongdoing. Let me know if you find any.'

Thus, Jack arrived at Fitzwarren Hall in the same car as Jamie Mackintosh who had given him a synopsis of the issues they were facing on the journey. Jack thought there was nothing left about the human condition to surprise him. Obviously, he'd been wrong. This situation had everything — birth, learning, emotion, aspiration, reason, morality, conflict, and death. In this job, you never stopped learning.

Beach let them in. 'Her Ladyship is waiting for you in the green reception room, gentlemen.'

They followed him down a long corridor to a room at the end where Beach tapped on the door before opening it. 'Mr Mackintosh and Detective Inspector Dawes to see you, my lady.' He retired immediately having lit the blue touch paper and being reluctant to witness the fireworks that would undoubtedly ensue.

'What's he doing here?' Helena pointed at Jack. 'I didn't give my permission for the police to interfere. I thought you'd come here to tell me about Hugo's Will, Mr Mackintosh. Why have you brought him?'

'Having seen the Will and some other documents left behind by His late Lordship, it transpires that there might be aspects of possible interest to the police.'

She stood up, still fretting that she'd had no message from Dickie and now angry that Hugo's Will may disadvantage her in some way. She needed money, and soon. The account that Hugo had set up for her was pretty much empty and now he was dead with the estate frozen, no more was coming in. Where the hell was Dickie?

'No! I'm not having this!' She threw back her long blonde hair in a gesture of rebellion. 'The contents of my late husband's Will are private to the Fitzwarrens. You can both go away and only come back, Mr Mackintosh, when you're ready to read it before the whole family.'

'When you hear what's in the other documents, Lady Helena, you might change your mind. There are some very personal revelations.' When she picked up the gin decanter, Jamie was almost preparing to duck.

She poured herself a hefty slug while she thought. What could Hugo have found out? He was a pompous little prick — always had been — but no great intellect. All the same, she could be on shaky ground. 'All right, Mr Mackintosh, you may stay, but the detective inspector can leave.'

Jack spoke for the first time. 'We can either do this here, Lady Helena, or I can take you down to the station and interview you under caution. It's up to you.'

That was the trigger for her to completely lose it. She went scarlet in the face and, for some moments, she couldn't breathe for outrage. 'How *dare* you speak to me like that! I want you to get out — now!' She gulped gin, neat.

Jack remained calm but decisive. 'In that case, Lady Helena, I'm arresting you on suspicion of—'

'I demand to speak to my solicitor . . . oh . . .' It was then she realized that her solicitor, Mackintosh, was already present and it was enough to disarm her temporarily. She sank down onto the sofa, thinking frantically.

Mackintosh took the opportunity, now that she'd shut up, to discuss what he'd really come for. 'Prior to his unfortunate demise, your late husband had been conducting genealogy tests on your children, Rupert and Charlotte.'

'What? Why? How?' Helena looked desperately from one man to the other. Things were taking a dangerous downturn. 'I don't understand.'

'To answer your questions one at a time — a genealogy test is a DNA based test used to verify relationships in families. As to why Lord Hugo was conducting these tests, it was because now that the children are adults, he had come to notice significant differences in their appearances. For example, His Lordship was short and of sallow colouring with brown hair and grey eyes; Rupert is very tall and has an olive complexion, black hair and dark eyes and Charlotte has auburn hair, green eyes and freckles. Of course, these features alone were not sufficient to confirm his suspicions, so he obtained DNA testing kits and surreptitiously carried out the procedures. When the results came back, they confirmed his worst fears — that neither Rupert nor Charlotte was his biological child.'

Jack took over the narrative. 'Given how important it was to Lord Hugo to continue the unbroken line of the Fitzwarrens, this was a devastating blow.'

'But what does it matter now?' Helena asked, panicking. 'They were born while Hugo and I were married.'

'You must see that it mattered a great deal to Hugo. So much so that he had given me instructions to file for divorce,' said Jamie. 'Also, his new Will completely disinherited you, Rupert and Charlotte.'

'The bastard said he'd never divorce me!' Helena was furious. 'So what am I supposed to live on? Who gets everything?' she demanded.

'Lord Hugo was planning to remarry after the divorce.'

'What? Over my dead body! Who was the scheming little tart?' Helena was turning white in the face with anger.

'I believe she was his personal assistant. He wanted someone young that he could be sure would provide him with a genuine heir.'

'Huh!' Helena let out a snarl of scornful laughter. 'That was never going to happen! Hugo was firing blanks and I can prove it. Two years into our marriage, when I didn't get pregnant and the drunken old Baron William was getting nasty and calling me Helena the Barren, I obtained a sample of Hugo's semen.'

'How?' asked Mackintosh.

'None of your business! I had it tested for sperm and guess what? No little swimmers — not even one. Knowing I'd be out on my ear if I didn't do something, I decided not to tell him. Instead, I renewed a friendship I'd had during my supermodelling career — a handsome Italian ski instructor from Cortina. I became pregnant with Rupert almost immediately and everyone was happy.' Her speech was becoming slurred. She looked at their expressions. 'You can think what you like! I haven't committed any crime.'

'What about Charlotte?' asked Jack. He had warmed to the young woman and feared she may be badly affected by these revelations. She had seemed genuinely fond of her 'Pa', even though, as it turned out, he was nothing of the sort.

'Poor Lottie was a mistake. I'm not sure who her father is — could have been one of the temporary under-gardeners. A horny-handed son of the soil, you might say.' She sniggered, drunkenly, waving her glass. 'I remember a big lad they called Ginger, because he had fiery auburn hair. It was probably him.'

Jack understood now what the legal implications were and why he was there. 'Do I understand you to say that you had Lord Hugo's name put on both birth certificates, knowing for certain that he wasn't the father?'

'Yes, of course I did. But it was years ago. What of it?'

'You can be charged with a crime which is alleged to have taken place years ago at any point in your life. Deliberately giving false details on a birth certificate is a criminal offence under the Perjury Act 1911 for which you can be sentenced to up to seven years in prison.'

She stared at him, her eyes failing to focus. Then she passed out.

CHAPTER SIXTEEN

'Blimey, that's put a spanner in the works,' said Bugsy. 'No heir to continue the Fitzwarren dynasty and no chance of ever producing one, now. Lord Hugo will be turning in his marble tomb.'

The incident room was buzzing with the fallout. 'Where does that leave our murder enquiry, sir?' asked Chippy.

'Exactly the same as it was before,' said Jack. 'Lord Hugo was murdered and it's our job to find out who did it.'

'What will happen to Lady Helena?' asked Gemma.

'She was charged with perjury and released under investigation,' said Jack. 'I don't expect she'll get a prison sentence, although you never know. Not our responsibility now. It's in the hands of the CPS. We need to focus on the murder. There was a point when I thought Helena may have been a suspect to stop Lord Hugo from signing the new Will, but it was obvious she didn't even know he'd made one, never mind the proposed divorce and this Céline Dubois person that he'd already lined up to step into her shoes.'

'Whose responsibility is it to tell Dowager Beatrice, Rupert and Charlotte?' wondered Aled.

'Not the police,' said Bugsy, firmly. 'It's an internal matter for the family and solicitors to sort out. I've no doubt there will be all kinds of problems with massive tax implications and deciding who gets what — if anything.'

'It also begs the question of who's going to pay the bills in the meantime,' remarked Clive. 'I've done a thorough investigation into the whole of the Fitzwarren finances and the situation's worse than grim. There's no equity left in Fitzwarren Hall and huge debts.'

'What about all the medieval artefacts?' asked Bugsy. 'They should be worth something.'

'They would be if they were genuine, Sarge. The solicitor got Bob Beach to do an inventory. Over time, Hugo had sold them off to collectors and replaced them with fakes — good ones, but still fakes. The Fitz Gallery is completely burnt out including the contents and Rupert didn't take out any insurance.'

'And as we know, the Serious Fraud guys are crawling over Fitzwarren & Napier-Smythe Asset Management and I can only guess what the results of that will be,' surmised Jack.

'The only part of the Fitzwarren estate that's doing well is the farm,' added Clive. 'The two-thousand-acres will have to be confiscated but the actual farm and surrounding land belongs to Charlotte. I found the deeds were made over to her by Lord Hugo some years ago, so it isn't subject to inclusion in the Fitzwarren estate. Of course, there won't be any money to subsidise rare breeding programmes, but otherwise it's more or less self-supporting.'

Jack was glad. At least Charlie would have a home looking after the animals she loves. 'What about the Dower House, Clive?'

'It'll have to be sold, I guess.'

'The old girl will have to move in with her boyfriend,' declared Bugsy.

'When people talk about the privileged aristocracy, Lord Hugo Fitzwarren, 27th Baron of Richington, didn't have a lot going for him, did he? His Baronial Hall is in hock to the bank, his business partner's cleaned out the company and done a runner and he finds out his kids aren't really his kids. Then to cap it all, someone clouts him on the head and drowns him. I'm quite glad I'm just an ordinary copper.'

'And we're still no closer to finding out who killed him and why,' Jack reminded everyone. 'There has to be some connection between the vandalized portrait of William Fitzwarren, the murder of Hugo Fitzwarren and the attempt on the life of Rupert Fitzwarren. But apart from an obvious dislike of three generations of Fitzwarren men, I can't work out what it is.'

* * *

Cynthia and Corrie were spending their Friday lunch break working out in the gym of the Kings Richington Fitness Centre, instead of eating their usual decadent, carb and fat laden meal in Chez Carlene. It had been Cynthia's idea.

Pedalling away on an exercise bike, Corrie gasped, 'Remind me. Why are we doing this?'

'Because I put on all that weight on the cruise,' Cynthia wheezed. 'And I'm not allowed to eat any of the lovely grub on Carlene's menu because I'm on a detox diet. Two weeks of bran, raw broccoli, and air freshener.'

Cynthia was rocking a purple, racerback sports bra and padded bike shorts with hardly a sign of excess weight as far as Corrie could see. She, in turn, had dug out an old pair of black yoga pants with tummy control panel and adjustable buttock clamps. Her baggy grey T-shirt bore the legend *Warning – May Contain Alcohol.*

Cynthia stopped pedalling and sat back in the saddle for a breather. 'George says the Fitzwarrens are potless, skint and soon to be declared bankrupt? Has Jack mentioned anything like that?'

Grateful for the excuse, Corrie stopped pedalling, too. 'No, Jack never tells me anything interesting. He says it might compromise police confidentiality, but he did say he'd had to go to Fitzwarren Hall to sit in on an interview with Lady Helena and her solicitor.'

'Really? I say, what japes! I bet I know what that was about — the ladies in my Luncheon Club say that Lord Hugo was a 'jaffa' — you know, seedless.'

'Honestly, Cyn, how could they possibly know that?' Corrie never failed to be shocked at what Cynthia's Ladies Luncheon Club found out. They seemed to have eyes and ears everywhere and the worrying part was that their rumours were nearly always right.

'It begs the question — who takes over the coronet and ermine? Not Rupert because he isn't Hugo's biological son.' Cynthia sighed. 'Pity, he is rather dishy. He'd look great in all the regalia, like a latter-day Larry Olivier in something Shakespearian.'

'More to the point, who inherits all the debt and tax liability?' asked Corrie. 'I wonder how HMRC will work that one out, if Hugo doesn't have an heir.

'Oh, they'll get it from somewhere. They always do. Maybe the old Dowager has a few millions salted away for a rainy day.'

'Come along now, ladies, get pedalling.' The fitness instructor interrupted their conversation. 'You're here to work out, not gossip. You'll thank me when you've got the glutes, quads, hamstrings and calves of a twenty-five-year-old.' They resumed pedalling furiously. The instructor put a hand over her nose as she passed behind Cynthia. 'Really, Mrs Garwood, that isn't what we mean by a burpee.'

* * *

'Jack, this may come as a shock but that stuff you hinted at the other night and forbade me to repeat to a living soul on pain of death is being widely discussed among Cynthia's Ladies Luncheon Club.'

'What?' Jack nearly dropped his bottle of craft beer. 'It can't be. It's not possible. Everyone was told it would jeopardize the murder investigation and trigger a whole raft of lawsuits if word got out about the Fitzwarrens' financial and familial disgrace. None of my team would have blabbed — they know better.'

'Well, I haven't said anything. It was Cyn who told me and I'm pretty certain George wouldn't have broken any rules so the police aren't the culprits.'

Jack groaned. 'At this rate, it'll be on the front page of the *Echo* before the end of the week. I can only guess that someone else saw those documents besides the Law Firm and Sir Barnaby.'

'But how could that happen?' asked Corrie. 'Didn't you say they were found by the butler in a locked briefcase down a priest hole and handed straight to Mackintosh?'

'Hmm.' Jack's brain was in the beehive groove again. When Jamie Mackintosh had handed over Hugo's phone that he'd kept hidden in the priest hole, Jack had given it to Clive to unlock. He'd discovered numerous messages of a romantic nature between him and Céline Dubois where Hugo promised her a life of luxury and prestige as the wife of an English baron. But more insistent were his requests for proof of her claim that she was a direct descendant of Ralph de Warren of St. Aubin le Cauf in Normandy and father of William de Warren, who he believed to be his own ancestor. Céline had clearly been carefully researched, located and selected to inject some vital new blood into the Fitzwarren line. Jack decided that he'd met a few fruit cakes in the line of duty, but the late Hugo Fitzwarren beat them all.

* * *

The official reading of the Will was a dismal affair. It took place in Jamie Mackintosh's office on a grey, rainy day and was attended by only seven people — Dowager Beatrice, Sir Leonard Montgomery who was there to support her, Helena, Rupert and Charlotte. Bob and Jessie Beach were also invited as they were mentioned briefly in Hugo's Will. Louise had been notified as an interested party, out of common courtesy, but had replied that she wanted no part of it and had no intention of coming down from Scotland, merely to witness the remaining Fitzwarrens all fighting to get their snouts in the trough. At that point, she had no way of knowing that the 'trough' was effectively empty and the 'snouts' were about to go hungry.

Mackintosh addressed the sparse assembly. 'Mrs Louise Fitzwarren has been contacted but has declined to attend.'

'Good,' croaked Rupert. 'That means she doesn't get any of the loot so there's all the more for us.' He was still very hoarse but claimed he had recovered sufficiently to leave his room in the private and very expensive hospital and the glamorous nurse who went with it, long enough to make sure he was properly taken care of in his father's Will.

For legal reasons, Jamie first read the terms of the original Will which left everything in the keeping of his heir, Lord Rupert Fitzwarren, 28th Baron of Richington, for his lifetime, to preserve for posterity and for the eventual perpetuation of the 29th baron. Various parcels of land, property and money went to the rest of the family and some members of staff. But Jamie was then obliged to tell them about the contents of the latest unsigned Will and the reasons the late Lord Hugo had given for the radical changes.

He took a deep breath. 'Following a series of tests carried out by His late Lordship, irregularities came to light regarding his DNA and that of Rupert and Charlotte.'

Helena's eyebrows shot up into her hairline. 'Mr Mackintosh—' she inclined her head towards Bob and Jessie — '*pas devant les domestiques.*'

Jamie ignored her. He was having none of her *arriviste* nonsense.

'What DNA?' asked Rupert, confused. 'What kind of 'irregularities'?'

'It means the tests showed they weren't a match. Lord Hugo wasn't your biological father.' Jamie was amazed that the information hadn't filtered down already. Despite every attempt to keep it under wraps, it had become a major topic of gossip among the *cognoscenti*. People like to see the mighty fallen and this revelation was a really juicy one. 'For that reason, neither Helena, Rupert nor Charlotte Fitzwarren are provided for in the new Will.'

'Yes, but he died before he could sign it,' protested Helena, 'so surely the first Will is the legal one.'

'That is correct, Lady Helena. The courts will not normally step in to order that an unexecuted Will should take effect, although it may take the deceased's intentions into account. However, in this particular case, circumstances render it irrelevant.' Then came the real bomb shell. 'Due to the outstanding debts and imminent tax liabilities, any monies realized from the sale of Fitzwarren Hall, the cars and boats and everything else that's saleable, will be swallowed up. The estate is insolvent. In other words, its assets are insufficient to meet its liabilities. The Fitzwarren estate must therefore be administered in terms of Section 34 of the Administration of Estates Act.'

The room, already cold and gloomy, seemed to get even gloomier as the afternoon closed in, the light faded and outside, it began to sleet.

'Mummy, what does he mean, there's no money?' whined Rupert, regressing, as he always did in times of trouble, to his pampered childhood. 'There must be money — otherwise what will I live on, now that the gallery's gone? I'm a peer of the realm, I have to be protected.'

'I'm afraid you aren't, my darling.' Helena took hold of his hand. 'Didn't you understand what Mackintosh just said? Hugo wasn't your father so you don't inherit the title.'

'Who is my father, then? Is he wealthy?' He sounded as hopeful as he was desperate.

'I doubt it, sweetheart. I haven't seen him for over twenty years and back then he was a young, handsome ski instructor living mainly off the proceeds of pleasuring rich women.'

'You mean my father was a — gigolo?' His face twisted with disgust. 'Women *paid* him for sex?'

'And skiing lessons, when he had the time. But he was wild, exciting and incredibly handsome, just like you, my

147

darling.' Helena stroked his hair but he pushed her off, furious.

'Why couldn't you have got pregnant by your husband?' He almost hissed the angry words. 'Then at least I'd still have the title and I could get credit on the strength of it.'

'Because Hugo was boring, mediocre and — sterile.' Helena spat out the last word, defiantly. 'Even his sperm wasn't up to the job.'

Lady Beatrice got up from her chair, walked across to Helena and slapped her hard across the face. 'You're a whore! My son should never have married a woman who paraded herself half-naked in magazines. I said as much at the time. Get out and take your two bastard brats with you!'

Sir Leonard pulled her away just as Helena stood up, braced to return the slap. 'Beatrice, don't make a spectacle of yourself. None of this is their fault.' He addressed the solicitor. 'Mr Mackintosh, what will happen to the Dower House?'

'It forms part of the estate so I'm afraid it will have to be sold to service the debts, along with everything else. I'm sorry.'

'You shall come and live with me, Beattie. There's plenty of room. We could get married if you like.' He put his arm around her trembling shoulders and led her away.

'Mr Mackintosh, what happens to the farm?' Charlotte asked, quietly. 'Does that have to be sold, too?'

At last, thought Jamie, relieved, *I can give someone some good news*. 'No, Miss Fitzwarren. It isn't part of the estate. Some time ago, Lord Hugo transferred the deeds to you to ensure you'd always have a home and that the Fitzwarren rare breeds that you love would endure, whatever else happened. It belongs to you so it can't be included.'

'Oh, I didn't know that. Pa never told me.' She brightened considerably. 'Thank you. Is it all right if I go now? I need to tell Adam and Dani that everything's going to be all right.'

'Don't you want to know who your real father might be?' snivelled Helena, nursing her inflamed cheek.

'No thank you, Mother. I really don't care who you slept with. It was Pa who looked after me and brought me up.' She gathered up her jacket and bag and left.

The only member of that family with any class, thought Jamie.

* * *

'Excuse us, Mr Mackintosh.' Bob Beach approached his desk. 'I guess this means Jessie and I are effectively unemployed. Should we begin looking for new positions?'

'I shouldn't be in too much of a hurry,' advised Jamie. 'There's a Middle-Eastern gentleman who's very interested in buying Fitzwarren Hall as an addition to his portfolio of global properties. I believe he intends to keep it exactly as it is — an example of a typically medieval part of British history and he plans to stay there when he and his international colleagues visit London on business. He has expressed a wish to retain all of the staff if possible. Shall I tell him that you would be prepared to stay?'

Bob looked at Jessie and she nodded, vigorously. 'Yes, please. Despite some of the unfortunate events that have occurred recently, we still consider it our home.'

'The buyer in question also wishes to keep the cars, especially the Bentley and Rolls Royce, so he'll want the services of a chauffeur. Perhaps you could mention it to Mr Carson.'

'Yes, of course. He'll be very pleased. He was only worrying the other day that he thought the family would have to let him go, as so few of them used the cars now.'

Once they'd all departed and his office was empty again, Jamie breathed a sigh of relief. He'd read many Wills in his time but none with quite such extreme repercussions as this one. He realized it had left him feeling drained. He went down the corridor to his father's office and tapped on the door.

'Come in, laddie. How did it go?' Angus had been expecting an update.

'About as badly as we anticipated, possibly worse.' Jamie sank down into the comfortable chair that Angus provided for visitors. 'It was harrowing enough having to reveal that Rupert and Charlie weren't Hugo's biological children but the worst part was telling them that the estate was insolvent.'

'How did they take it?' Angus took out the bottle of single malt and poured a shot for his son.

'Rupert whined on like a toddler, moaning about where his allowance was going to come from and blaming his mother for everything going tits-up, and then Helena and Beatrice came to blows.'

'Really? That bad?'

'Yes, and I never got around to telling them about Mlle Dubois who, I have since discovered, has legged it back to France, taking with her a sizeable chunk of Fitzwarren cash. It had been settled on her by Hugo in exchange for an affidavit promising to marry him as soon as the divorce was finalized.'

'Why the blazes did he do that?'

'When I questioned the affidavit, he blethered on about the Fitzwarren stock needing the reintroduction of Normandy blood. I'm telling you, Dad, the bloke was borderline bonkers.'

'Most of the aristocracy are laddie. It's all the inbreeding.'

Jamie sighed. 'It's probably just as well that it's the end of the line for the Fitzwarrens.'

CHAPTER SEVENTEEN

'Thank you, Monty, I appreciate the offer, but I don't want to come and live with you.' Beatrice was resolute. 'I'm too set in my ways and I'm not used to sharing my personal space with someone else.'

They were having sherry and sponge fingers in the Dower House after the stressful events of the day. A log in the fire crackled and sparks flew, emphasizing Beatrice's prickly response.

'But, Bea, how will you manage?' Leonard wondered if she fully understood her situation. 'You heard what Mackintosh said, the estate is insolvent. There's no more money coming in. The creditors will get everything. Soon, you won't have a space at all.'

'Yes, I know, I'm not stupid. But if I can raise enough cash, I intend to buy the Dower House when it comes up for sale.'

'And how will you do that?' asked Monty, with just a hint of sarcasm. 'You've always claimed that you haven't much capital.'

'I haven't, but I soon will have. I'm going to sell the Fitzwarren sapphires.' She said it in a manner that brooked no argument.

Leonard couldn't disguise his shock. 'But Beattie, you can't. They're not yours to sell. They belonged to William's grandmother so they're heirlooms — part of the Fitzwarren estate.'

'Tosh!' Beatrice exclaimed. 'I'm going to sell them and before you ask, I've already found a dealer in the city.'

'That will be in Hatton Garden. I know some business people there. If you're determined to do this, will you at least allow me to escort you?'

'No thank you, Monty. And anyway, my dealer isn't in Hatton Garden, he's in a place called Tower Hamlets. I think that's what it's called. I have the address written down somewhere. It sounds like a very pleasant community of little villages.'

Sir Leonard was deeply concerned. Despite her advancing years, Beatrice was an innocent, having had little exposure to what he regarded as the 'real' world. It was one of the things about her that had attracted him — her obvious need for his protection. 'How did you find out about this dealer?'

'From an old friend who is sadly no longer with us. After William gave me the sapphires, this friend suggested that if I ever fell upon hard times, this address is where I could sell them. At the time, I believed he was joking and I hadn't given it a thought until now, but I have indeed fallen upon hard times. I just hope this jewel company he mentioned is still trading after all these years. I shall get Carson to drive me there tomorrow, so I shall be quite safe. Now, don't fuss and pour me another sherry.'

* * *

George Carson didn't bat an eyelid when the Dowager summoned him next day and handed him the piece of paper with the East London address on it.

'Carson, I need you to drive me there and wait for me. I have some business to attend to. It may take some time.'

'Very well, my lady.'

She frowned. 'You do know where this is, I hope? It's important.'

'Oh yes, my lady. I was born and brought up in Tower Hamlets. I know the area very well.'

'Good.' She put the jewel case containing the sapphires into her bag. 'I'm ready. Please bring the car round.'

The traffic was bad and it was some time before they finally reached the destination. Carson eased the Bentley down an empty urban back street, grim and foreboding, then turned into an alley lined with deserted buildings, the windows boarded up and broken, with rubbish spewing out of bins and skinny cats running for cover. He pulled up outside a dirty, splintered door covered in graffiti — it was the address that Beatrice had given him. If she had been expecting a glitzy showroom with a glass front and elegant signage, she was disappointed.

'This is it, my lady.' He opened the car door for her. 'Would you like me to come in with you?'

'No, Carson, that won't be necessary.' She didn't want one of the servants to witness what she was doing. It would be common knowledge in a flash and this transaction had to be kept secret. She stepped out, then hesitated. 'You are sure this is the right place?' She found it difficult to believe that this place had the pretty name of Tower Hamlets, nor that she was in the same borough as the vibrant, thriving hub of Canary Wharf where Monty had taken her to dinner occasionally.

'Yes, I'm quite sure, my lady.' He put his shoulder to the rotten wooden door, jammed into a warped frame and shoved it open. Then he stood back to let her pass through.

It was gloomy inside with a single lamp hanging from the ceiling. The room stank of cigarettes, unwashed bodies and general decay. A man in a shabby overall emerged from a back room where a large dog was barking and hurling itself at the door, trying to escape. The man yelled to it to shut up then looked Beatrice up and down, taking in the expensive clothes and fancy head gear at a glance.

'Whatever it is you're looking for, love, you're in the wrong place. Shut the door on your way out.' He made to return to the back room.

'No, I don't think I am.' Beatrice sounded braver than she felt. 'I understand you buy jewellery.'

'Who told you that?' he snapped. His eyes narrowed warily.

'A friend.' She took out the case containing the sapphire necklace, earrings and bracelet, opened it and placed it on the counter between them. 'These sapphires come from Kashmir and they are very valuable.'

The man's eyes glinted with greed. He took a gemstone loupe from his pocket, screwed it into his eye to get a better look and examined each sapphire in turn. Finally, he spoke. 'This junk has never been anywhere near Kashmir. More like a stall in Camden Market. They're not sapphires, they're cheap paste. Bugger off, you daft old bat and stop wasting my time.'

'No! You're mistaken. You must be. They're worth a fortune.' She began to panic, seeing the prospect of keeping her home disappear into nothing. 'You're just saying that so you can beat me down on the price.'

He put the necklace flat on the table, picked up a half empty whiskey bottle and smashed it down on one of the stones. It shattered into dust. 'Now do you believe me? Push off before I set the dog on you.'

Beatrice grabbed what had turned out to be worthless costume jewellery and fled.

'Is everything all right, my lady?' Carson asked politely, when she came staggering out to the car.

'No, it isn't,' Beatrice sobbed. 'Take me home at once.'

The whole experience had been exhausting. The worst part was realizing that Hugo must have replaced her sapphires with fakes some time ago to service the overwhelming Fitzwarren debts. Back in the warmth and safety of the Bentley with a rug over her, Beatrice eventually fell into an uneasy sleep. When she woke, Carson had parked outside an abandoned warehouse on the docks. The light was fading fast and all she could see was the derelict building and below, the cold, dark river.

154

'What's the matter?' she asked, befuddled with sleep. 'Why have we stopped? Have we broken down?'

'No.' He opened the door, grasped her arm and pulled her out. In his other hand, he held a coil of rope that he'd taken from the boot.

'Carson! What are you doing? Why are we here?'

'Because you and I are going to have a chat, my lady, and the name's George Barnes. Carson was my mother's maiden name.'

'Barnes? I don't understand. That was the name of . . .'

'Your chauffeur — Sid Barnes. That's right. The man that your drunken husband, William, killed fifteen years ago. Come along.' He half dragged her inside the rickety, damp warehouse. The rotting building, with its peeling paint and exposed brickwork, had an atmosphere of decay and abandonment. Most of the windows had been smashed, leaving shards of glass scattered all over the floor.

'Carson — Barnes — whatever your name is. Stop this at once! Let go my arm.' Beatrice tried to struggle but his grip was firm. 'I don't know what you think you're doing but if you don't stop it immediately and drive me home, I shall report you to the police.' Her words sounded imperious but she was frightened. 'I don't want to have a chat. It's getting dark. I demand you take me home.'

'Sorry, Beatrice old girl, but for once in your entitled life, you don't get to give the orders.' Once inside the warehouse, George pushed her down onto a dirty, broken chair and dropped the coil of rope he was carrying onto the floor beside her. 'Now, be quiet and listen for a change. I'm going to tell you a story.'

Beatrice was very scared. Carson had always been so polite, so obedient and deferential. The perfect servant. She wondered if he was having some kind of breakdown and had gone completely mad. In the end, she thought it safer to do what he wanted until she could get away. She had no idea where they were and her mobile phone was in her bag in the back of the car. There had been no sign of anyone on the deserted dockside when he dragged her in, so there was no point in screaming for help and she doubted if she could summon the breath anyway.

George began to walk around her in threatening circles, like a lone wolf assessing his prey. 'Are you sitting comfortably, Beatrice? No? Well, never mind, I'll begin anyway. Once upon a time, there was a baron called William Fitzwarren who lived in a magnificent stately home. He had a wife, Beatrice, a son, Hugo, and lots of money that he hadn't had to work his arse off to earn, like everybody else. He should have been very happy. But he was a tyrant and a bully and he drank too much. He had a nasty temper that he took out on anybody who crossed him because he was used to getting his own way.'

'That isn't true . . .' whimpered Beatrice.

'Shut up! I didn't say you could interrupt.' George shouted in her face and she could feel his hot breath on her cheek. 'One day, Baron William told his chauffeur, Sid, that he wanted to go down the river in his motorboat, so they set off. But after a while, William insisted on taking over the wheel himself, even though he was shitfaced — that means 'very drunk' in your posh English, Your Ladyship. Sid tried to stop him — they struggled and lost control of the boat. It hit a bridge and burst into flames killing them both. At the inquest, the coroner was persuaded that it was Sid Barnes who was drunk although everyone knew he was teetotal and had never touched alcohol in his life.'

'You don't know that's what happened,' protested Beatrice, sticking out her chin. 'Nobody does.'

'Maybe not for sure but that's what William's son, Lord Hugo wanted everyone to believe. He couldn't allow the honour of the Fitzwarrens to be besmirched in any way. And because he was a baron, people went along with the lie.'

'Carson — I mean, George — I can't do anything about it now. It happened fifteen years ago.'

'No, but you could have done something at the time. Sid Barnes, in case you haven't guessed, was my father. After your husband killed him, my mother was left alone with me to bring up. I was just a kid. She had no family of her own and her health was poor. We were destitute so she came to you asking for help and you turned her away.'

'That wasn't me, it was Hugo!' Beatrice gabbled, desperately trying to vindicate herself. 'He said if we gave her money, it would look like an admission of guilt.'

George ignored that and carried on with his story. 'After Mother was driven to an early grave by overwork, exhaustion and malnutrition, I vowed to bring down the House of Fitzwarren. Punish everyone who was part of the conspiracy of silence and, most importantly, put an end to the unbroken family line that made your son so proud. The irony is that Helena had already done that by 'breeding out' — isn't that what they call it in aristocratic circles?' He laughed unpleasantly. 'So I didn't need that clumsy attempt to roast Rupert alive, after all. He wasn't even a legitimate Fitzwarren. I was sorry about the girl, though. Wrong place, wrong time.' He put his face up close to hers. 'That just leaves you, Dowager, and you're the worst of them.'

'Oh my God, it was you!' Beatrice put a hand to her mouth in horror. 'You murdered Hugo and set fire to the gallery.' She could feel her heart pounding in her chest and her breath rasped from her throat.

'Well done, old lady. You've finally got the message and I've nearly completed what I set out to do.' He paced up and down. 'It hasn't been easy, you know, kowtowing to a bunch of dim-witted narcissists with an exaggerated sense of their own importance — having to be servile to deluded idiots who expect to be recognized as superior even without any achievements to justify it — just an accident of birth.' He stood facing her. 'And now it's nearly over and I'm glad.' He pointed. 'Do you see that trapdoor over there? It drops straight down into the Thames. Back in the day, dockers used it as a quick way to get rid of their rubbish. Chuck it down there and you never see it again. Of course, nobody comes here anymore, only the rats and pigeons. In a day or so, when I'm ready,

157

I'm going to shove you down that trapdoor and into the river but I don't want them to find you too soon. When they do find you — if they find you — you'll have decomposed into a slimy, half-eaten collection of body parts, like your precious son. In the meantime,' he picked up the rope and began to tie her shaking arms and legs to the filthy chair, 'you can stay here. And try not to die — I want you to have plenty of time to think about your past misdeeds while I drive back to Fitzwarren Hall in the Bentley.' He pulled out a roll of duct tape and stuck it over her mouth. 'I shall tell anyone who asks that I took you to the address you gave me and that you told me not to wait as you'd made alternative travel arrangements, so I drove back home, put the Bentley away and went to bed. And that's exactly what I'm going to do now. Goodbye for the time being, Beattie, dear.' He blew her a kiss. 'See you soon.'

* * *

When Jack's phone rang at midnight, he was already in bed. He knew Corrie had spent a long day at Coriander's Cuisine preparing the food for a big leaving do at Richington Local Authority and she needed her sleep. He grabbed his phone and stopped it ringing, hoping not to wake her but she was a light sleeper and sat up immediately.

'Who's that at this time of night? — as if I didn't know.' She guessed who it was without Jack telling her.

'Dawes? This is DCS Garwood. Listen carefully, this is important.'

Typical, thought Jack. *Not so much as a 'sorry to disturb you so late at night' or any of the other pleasantries that normal people would use.* 'Good evening, sir. Do we have a problem?'

'Too bloody right, we do.'

Jack guessed that would be the royal 'we' and what he actually meant was that Jack had the problem, so he expected Jack to deal with it.

'The Commander has contacted me. He had a call from Angus Mackintosh, who was contacted by his son, Jamie, who'd had an emergency call from Sir Leonard Montgomery. Are you keeping up, Dawes?'

'Yes, I think so, sir.' Jack was once again reminded of the trajectory of managerial excrement.

'It seems that the Dowager Fitzwarren went out today to one of the less salubrious parts of our city and she still hasn't returned. Sir Leonard is concerned because she isn't answering her phone and, apparently, she rarely stays out after eight o'clock at this time of year. Added to which, she has a very serious heart complaint and could fall off her perch at any time.'

'Do we know what she went out to do, sir?' Jack was already out of bed and looking for his trousers.

'Well, that's the tricky part and it's why Sir Leonard didn't just dial 999 straight off but went through more convoluted channels. As I understand it, Lady Beatrice was intending to sell the Fitzwarren sapphires.'

'Can she do that, sir? I imagine they're a family heirloom and part of the Fitzwarren estate. I thought everything had to go when you're declared insolvent.'

'Never mind the financial protocols now, Dawes. The issues we need to address are where she's gone and why she hasn't come back. The police involvement is because it sounds like she was attempting to do a deal with some seedy fence, a receiver of stolen goods, not a bona fide jeweller. Whoever it is has probably got form and can be traced through police records.'

'Right, sir. What do you want me to do?'

'Well, first off, find the car, obviously. Use your initiative, man. The chauffeur drove her to the location in a bloody great Bentley. I shouldn't imagine you'd find many Bentleys in that part of the manor — not with the wheels still on it, anyway. Get moving and find the bloody woman before she drops dead and the press, her MP, social media, IOPC and Uncle Tom Cobley get wind of it and blame the police.'

'OK, sir. I'm on it.' Jack looked at his watch and wondered if he would be exceeding his authority if he rang Clive.

On the other hand, he knew his Digital Forensic Specialist was a nerd of the first order, so he probably spent half the night designing highly complex computer games. It was while he was punching in the number that Jack realized he didn't even know if Clive had a partner.

As if confirming Jack's thoughts about burning the midnight oil, Clive answered straight away. 'Sir? Do you need me?'

'Yes, Clive, and I'm really sorry to trouble you at this time of night but can you remember if we ever did a background check on George Carson?'

'That'll be the Fitzwarrens' chauffeur. No sir, I don't believe we did because he'd only been employed by them for a year and we were looking at employees who might have a long-term grudge. Do you want me to do one now?'

'Yes please, Clive. An old lady's life's in danger, otherwise I wouldn't ask. I'll be at the station.'

'I'm on my way.'

CHAPTER EIGHTEEN

When Jack got to the station, the redoubtable Sergeant Parsloe was working the graveyard shift on the desk.

'Blimey, Jack, couldn't you sleep? You haven't been gone five minutes. I don't think the overnight cleaners have finished in your room yet.'

'That's OK, Norman. There'll just be the two of us — me and Clive.'

'Not quite,' grinned Norman as the door opened to admit not only Clive but Aled, Gemma, Chippy and Velma all showing the results of hastily-thrown-on clothes.

'What are you lot doing here?' Jack never ceased to be impressed by the uncanny level of communication between his officers.

'Clive reckoned you could do with a few more pairs of hands, sir,' said Gemma.

'So here we are,' confirmed Aled. 'What's occurring, sir?' A form of enquiry frequently used by his mates in his home town of Pontypool and still came naturally to him.

Jack was about to explain when the door opened and a dishevelled Sergeant Malone shambled in, finishing off a slice of toast and marmalade. He wiped sticky fingers down his trousers. 'Evening all.'

'Is that a pyjama top under your jacket, Sarge?' grinned Gemma.

'It might be, DC Fox. I was in a hurry. What's going on?'

Clive had clearly sent out an all-MIT bulletin — *either that*, thought Jack, *or they're all bloody telepathic like the Midwich Cuckoos!* They trooped up to the incident room, bickering about whose turn it was to make the coffee.

The cleaners had just finished and were gathering up their equipment. 'Haven't you people got homes to go to?' asked the team leader. 'And whichever one of you keeps chucking bits of mouldy food in the waste bins, please don't. It attracts the rats.'

Bugsy assumed a wide-eyed look of innocence and nobody grassed him. 'What are we looking at, guv?' he asked, when the last cleaner had left and closed the door behind her.

Jack filled them in with what he knew so far. It took some time. Then finally: 'The last known whereabouts of Dowager Beatrice was when the chauffeur, Carson, drove her in the Bentley to an address in the East End. We need to locate the Bentley first off. Put out an ANPR check.' Jack hoped a check of the Automatic Number Plate Recognition cameras might at least give an idea of the car's location and the route it had travelled to get there.

Minutes later, Aled called out, 'Sir, I just phoned Bob Beach to get the Bentley's registration. He asked why I wanted it so I told him we needed to establish the car's whereabouts. He said, 'That's easy. It's in the garage. Carson brought it back some hours ago.'

'What about Lady Beatrice?'

'Mr Beach said he'd assumed Carson had dropped her at the Dower House.'

'So where is Carson now?' asked Bugsy.

'He's in his flat above the garage, Sarge. Apparently, Mrs Beach was preparing to take him a cup of early morning tea.'

'Get uniform to pull him in,' ordered Jack.

* * *

George Carson was remarkably reasonable about being woken up and brought into Richington nick by two uniformed police officers. He had confirmed his ID and got into the police car without any protest. PC 'Johnny' Johnson expressed the opinion to Sergeant Parsloe that George seemed like a 'really nice bloke'. Nothing like the gobshites that they were usually sent to pick up at that time of the morning. Carson had given them no trouble at all. Once he was safely in the interview room, Sergeant Parsloe gave him a cup of tea to make up for the one he said he'd just missed at Fitzwarren Hall.

'Thank you, Sergeant. Very kind of you.'

'That's OK, son. Inspector Dawes will be down to speak to you very soon.'

* * *

'Any luck with the background check, Clive, before I go down to question him?' Jack asked.

'No, sir.' He looked defeated which was unusual for the techie geek who rarely let anything beat him. 'It's strange but I couldn't find anything on him before the age of seventeen when he passed his driving test. I'm guessing he must have had a different name. Since then, he has no form, pays his NI and tax in his job as chauffeur with the Fitzwarrens and has a credit card that he pays off in full at the end of every month. Squeaky clean. A model citizen. No traffic offences, nothing of any note at all.'

'OK, Clive. Sergeant Malone and I will try to get some answers.'

When they entered the interview room, Carson was dunking a rich tea biscuit that Sergeant Parsloe had conjured up from somewhere.

Jack smiled affably. 'Thank you for coming in, Mr Carson, especially at this unsocial hour.'

The usual response from suspects at this point was: *'Didn't have a bloody choice, did I? Two sodding great coppers dragged*

163

me out of bed and frogmarched me here.' But not Carson. 'Not a problem, Inspector. What can I do to help?'

'We understand from Sir Leonard Montgomery that you drove the Dowager Lady Beatrice into the city yesterday.'

George's face took on an expression of deep concern. 'Yes, I did, and I don't mind telling you, I wasn't at all happy about it, sir.'

'Why was that?' asked Bugsy.

'Her Ladyship gave me the address and it was in an area that I knew was far from safe for a lady to visit. But she employs me and I felt I had no option but to do what she wanted.'

'Can you tell us where this place is?' Jack wanted to know.

'Oh yes, sir. I can write it down for you.' Bugsy handed him his notebook and he carefully wrote down the address and handed it back.

'What happened when you got there?'

'Well, it turned out to be a broken-down workshop in one of the more deprived areas of East London. I couldn't understand why Her Ladyship wanted to go there. I asked her if I could go in with her but she wouldn't let me, so I waited outside in the car. I didn't like the place at all and I was tempted to disobey her and insist, but she could be stubborn and I didn't want to lose my job.'

'What happened after that?' There was no doubt about it, thought Bugsy. This bloke would make a very credible witness if it came to that.

'I waited for what must have been an hour and I could hear raised voices and a dog barking. I was about to knock and ask if everything was all right, when Her Ladyship came out. She told me not to wait as she had more business to conduct and it could take some hours. She'd made other travel arrangements, she said, and she didn't need me. Then she went back in and shut the door. I wondered if I ought to wait anyway but she seemed very determined. So I drove back to Fitzwarren Hall, put the car away and went to bed, but I wasn't at all comfortable with the situation. I hope I didn't do wrong, sir.'

Jack and Bugsy exchanged glances. 'The reason we're worried, Mr Carson, is that Lady Beatrice didn't come home to the Dower House and nobody knows where she is.'

'I blame myself!' Carson seemed genuinely distressed. 'I should never have left her there. In fact, I shouldn't have taken her there in the first place but with Lord Hugo gone, there really isn't anyone in charge now. That area is home to all sorts of violent criminals. What will you do to find her, Inspector?'

'Don't upset yourself, Mr Carson. We'll find her,' Bugsy assured him.

* * *

The cameras confirmed Carson's account of his journey along the main roads, but not surprisingly, the area he described was something of a black hole in terms of surveillance and they lost him, both on the way in and back out. But once he was back within ANPR, they could see that he was on his own in the car. The breakthrough came when Jack contacted his old colleague Mike from the City Police.

'Blimey, Jack, you never call, you never write — nothing for weeks and now I suppose you've run out of mates and you're missing me.'

Jack laughed. 'Mike, you're a berk. Listen, what do you know about a fence specializing in high-end jewellery in the Tower Hamlets area?' He read out the address.

'Hang on a minute. I'll shout up. We've got thief-takers here with memories that go way back.'

Jack could hear conversations going on in the back-ground then Mike came back. 'Apparently, we were aware of activity years back, but there's been nothing recent. We assumed that the perps had moved on when it got too hot for them to operate. Are you saying the racket has started up again?'

'Could be, Mike. But it isn't just the racket that we're interested in. Remember the Fitz Gallery that burned down on your patch?'

'How could I forget? The nightclub and the insurance companies are still fighting over who has financial responsibility and demanding to know why we haven't caught the arsonist yet.'

'Well, the Dowager Beatrice is the grandmother of Rupert Fitzwarren, gallery owner and putative 28th Baron of Richington.'

'Why is he only putative?' Mike asked.

'It's complicated. Anyway, the Dowager was last seen going in to that Tower Hamlets address but not coming out and because she's nobility, top brass are freaking out.'

'Bloody hell! Do you mean the old girl's disappeared?'

'Effectively, Mike, yes. She dismissed her chauffeur saying she'd arranged alternative transport. He's pretty cut up about it. Blames himself for leaving her there.'

'What the hell was she doing in a location like that in the first place?'

'Trying to sell the family jewels, apparently.'

'Of course. Silly me. Why else would a Dowager Baroness go to a godforsaken shithole in the arse end of London if not to flog a few heirlooms? Why don't we mount a joint initiative, Jack, and pay them a surprise visit? If she's in there, we'll find her.'

'That's what I was hoping you'd say.'

* * *

Given the lack of knowledge about the size of the operation, and since there was no time to carry out a full risk assessment, it was decided to deploy SCO–19, a specially trained 'SWAT' team of heavily armed firearms officers operating under the Metropolitan Police. Their job was to diffuse high-risk situations. Records had shown that the previous gang, who once operated from the address but who were since thought to be disbanded, had been armed and extremely dangerous, so they were taking no chances.

At the appointed time, several large, unmarked vehicles pulled into the empty back street and officers wearing helmets, body armour, shields and gas masks piled out. Jack and Mike stayed well back to observe but not get involved. The officers, spearheaded by the SCO-19 Special Firearms Officers, crept into the alley in a disciplined column and ducked beneath the windows for cover. On the leader's command, the SFOs stormed the address, throwing in stun grenades and a tear gas cannister. An officer with a heavy-duty dog pole stood by to capture the dog that was reported to be inside. An ambulance was on standby to deal with any casualties including the vulnerable elderly lady with the heart condition who was allegedly being held captive.

The officer with the 'enforcer' or 'big red door key' as it was familiarly known, stepped forward and smashed down the splintering door with one strike. There was a great deal of shouting as they barged their way inside, calling for the occupants to show themselves. The dog, a big, muscular pit bull, rushed barking and growling to attack the nearest officer but was safely caught in the loop of the dog pole, led away and put in a van. The men went into each stinking room at a time shouting 'clear' when no one emerged.

Watching from a safe distance, Jack was impressed by the military precision of the operation but disappointed that there was no sign of Lady Beatrice and nobody had yet been brought out in handcuffs. Just as he was starting to give up hope, he spotted a man climbing over the fence at the back of the house and out of sight of the SFOs.

'Mike, look! Chummy's getting away.' Jack pointed.

'Quick, let's grab him.' He grinned. 'Christ, Jack! This is like old times.'

They both leaped out of the car and shot off in hot pursuit. They caught up with him fifty metres down the road and wrestled him to the ground.

He capitulated. 'All right. Give over. You wouldn't have caught me only I copped a lungful of that gas.'

'Where are the others?' demanded Mike, breathless from the unaccustomed exercise and deciding he was too old for this lark.

'What others? There aren't any others. Just me.'

* * *

The SFOs returned to base and the operation was closed down. They had found some odds and sods of jewellery and silver inside the house but nothing of any real value and as the leader of the operation had pointed out somewhat caustically, they didn't find any 'distressed old ladies'.

Jack sat in when Mike and his sergeant questioned their only prisoner, a chancer called Vince. At that point, it wasn't clear what they could charge him with — if anything.

'The word on the street, Vince, is that you're a fence — a receiver of stolen goods,' accused Mike. 'That's against the law.'

'Who? Me?' He sounded hurt at the very suggestion. 'I don't know who you've been talking to Inspector, but you've got it all wrong. I'm not a fence. All right, I buy and sell a few items. What you have to understand, gentlemen, are the socio-economic factors that create this type of environment. Folk round here need an extra few quid on top of what they blag off the government in unemployment benefits, so they nick stuff and bring it to me. It's their side hustle. I help them out by selling it on. You could say I'm a Community Development Worker. I help individuals, families and often whole communities to bring about social change and improve the quality of life in their local deprived area. It's called levelling-up.'

'You're full of bullshit, Vince. Do you know that?' said Mike. 'How did you get into the business of 'community development' in the first place?'

'Ah well, that would be down to my old dad — no longer with us, God rest him. He started the business from the very workshop that your lot just trashed. Rumour has it that he helped fence some of the stones from the Antwerp diamond job. "Heist of the century" they called it. The family was very proud.'

'What have you done with the elderly lady?' asked Jack, bluntly.

Vince looked baffled for a few moments then it dawned. 'You mean the posh old bird who came in with a load of hooky sapphires?'

'Yes, that's the one,' said Jack. 'Where is she?'

'No idea, squire. Once I demonstrated that she'd been shafted by whoever it was who sold them to her, she buggered off in a strop.'

'Did you see where she went?' Jack was inclined to believe him.

'Yeah. She got into a bloody great Bentley and her chauffeur drove away. Now, what about a cup of tea and a few biscuits while you decide you haven't got enough evidence to charge me?'

CHAPTER NINETEEN

When Jack arrived back at Richington nick, he was in two minds about whose story to believe. George Carson, the hardworking, caring chauffeur who was deeply concerned about having left Dowager Beatrice in danger, or Vince, the career crook who had dismissed her as a posh old bird who'd buggered off in a strop. The conundrum was soon to be resolved.

'Guv, Big Ron wants to see us.' Bugsy announced. 'She says it's important.'

'OK, let's go.' Jack hoped this would be the answer he desperately needed.

Dr Hardacre was in the laboratory examining the helmet from the suit of armour that had been forced onto Lord Hugo's head before he was shoved into the Thames.

'Ah, Inspector, there you are. I need you to look at this.' She stretched out her hand and her assistant, Miss Catwater, compliant as ever, put a petri dish in it. 'This was on the very edge of the helmet and I almost missed it. Do you know what it is?'

Jack peered closely at the barely visible, black oleaginous smudge. 'No, Doctor. Sorry.'

'What about you, Sergeant?' she challenged.

Bugsy put on his reading glasses. 'It looks like oil to me, Doc. Possibly engine oil?'

'Well done, Sergeant. Ten out of ten. I've tested it and that's exactly what it is. Now, who among your list of suspects is most likely to have been in contact with engine oil?' She beamed as they both made for the door. 'You can thank me later,' she called after them.

'Thanks, Doctor,' Jack called back. 'Rustle up some uniforms, Bugsy. We need to pick him up before he finishes off the last of the Fitzwarrens.'

* * *

Jack and Bugsy made it to Fitzwarren Hall in record time with considerable uniform backup. PC 'Johnny' Johnson and his colleagues took George Carson's flat apart but all his possessions had gone. It was immaculate, as if he had never been there.

Jack and Bugsy clattered hastily down to the kitchen where Jessie Beach was making tea.

'Hello, officers. What can I do for you? Would you like a cup of tea?'

'Not just now, thanks,' said Jack. 'Have you seen George Carson?'

'Yes, he just went out. What do you need him for? Perhaps Bob or I could help.'

'What about Lady Beatrice?' demanded Bugsy.

Jessie was bewildered about why they were asking all the questions. 'She's at home in the Dower House, isn't she? I expect she's busy packing. The Dower House is having to be sold to pay creditors but I expect you know that.'

'Do you know which car Carson took?' insisted Jack.

She dithered, trying to think. 'He didn't take a car, he went out on his motorcycle, but why . . . ?'

'He has a motorbike?' Jack and Bugsy shouted in unison.

'That's right. He goes for rides into the city on it, on his days off. Is it important?'

'Yes, Mrs Beach. It's very important.' Jack reckoned they should have guessed after the arson attack on the Fitz Gallery by a man on a motorbike. 'Do you know the registration number?'

'Not off the top of my head but there's a list of the number plates of all the vehicles kept at Fitzwarren Hall, hanging on the wall in the garage.'

'Please text the number of Carson's bike to me at the station. If he comes back, keep him here. By force if necessary. I'll leave a couple of uniformed officers with you.' The two detectives rushed off leaving her totally alarmed.

'Oh, my goodness! I must go and warn Bob.'

* * *

It was all systems go in the incident room with everyone on red alert.

'Do you think Lady Beatrice is still alive, sir?' Gemma asked cautiously.

'I don't know, Gemma, but we have to proceed as if she is.' Jack called across to Aled. 'Check ANPR. We need to know where Carson is and fast. It's my guess that he's gone back to wherever he was holding her to dispose of her body.'

'If he's killed her, won't he have done that already?' asked Aled.

'Possibly.' Jack had to accept that she could already be beyond help. 'But he won't have wanted her body to be found too soon, before he's had a chance to cover his tracks, establish an alibi and be a long way away.'

'Sir, once we realized that it was Carson who wrote KILLER on the portrait of Lord William, I followed a hunch and carried out a background check on him under the name of Barnes,' said Clive. 'And guess what — he's the son of Sid Barnes, the Fitzwarren's chauffeur who died in the boating accident alongside Lord William. The crash left just George and his sickly mother, Eileen, and she died not long after. He was born and brought up in Tower Hamlets so he'll know his way around the area.'

172

'Now it's starting to make sense,' said Bugsy. 'This is a case of long, drawn-out revenge. A deliberate attempt to put an end to the entitled family that he blames for the death of his dad and by association, his mum, too.'

'There were psychological clues in the methods he used but I didn't pick up on them,' lamented Velma. 'Fire and water because that's how his father died and the suit of armour helmet — a symbol of the virtuous family history which was a sham. Fat lot of use I am as a behavioural analyst.'

'Don't beat yourself up, Velma,' said Jack. 'None of us picked it up. I should have had a very early clue when my wife questioned why, if the killer was a political activist, he'd painted KILLER on William's portrait instead of something like FASCIST. But now I can see that it wasn't a political comment at all, it was an indictment.'

* * *

The A13 is a three-lane dual carriageway from Canary Wharf to the M25, which, in turn, connects to all the main routes into and out of London. Number Plate Recognition cameras caught up with the motorcycle entering the docklands area and then lost it again in the spider's web of the urban side roads. At times, it seemed as if every police officer in the area was out looking for George Barnes alias Carson.

Beatrice was alive but only just. Within the confused recesses of her fading mind, she wondered vaguely if Carson was coming back to finish her off or if she would simply pass away where she sat, to be discovered as a crumbling skeleton, years later. As if in answer, the door to the rickety warehouse slid open.

'Hello Beatrice. How are you doing? I'm back, like I promised.' He had parked the bike with its paniers full of his basic belongings, out front. He'd decided it was unlikely that anyone would notice and even if they did, they wouldn't care. He pulled the tape off her mouth.

'Water,' wailed Beatrice. 'Please . . . I need water.'

'Oh, you'll soon have plenty of that,' sneered George. 'But don't worry, love, it'll be quick. The water's around thirteen metres deep just here and at this time of year, it's bloody cold. Your dodgy heart will stop in minutes. You see, I don't want you to show any signs of foul play, when they find your body. It'll end up somewhere down the four kilometres that this part of the dockland stretches. That way, the authorities will just think you got lost, had a dizzy turn and fell in. And by then I shall be sunning myself on a beach somewhere. After all, there's no reason for me to stay here, since your family effectively wiped out all of mine. And soon, I'll have finished off what's left of yours. You must admit, it's the most perfect *schadenfreude*. You'll know what that means, you being an educated lady. You see, I didn't get much education on account of I had to work from a young age to support my ailing mother. Now, here's what we're going to do next, my lady, before I chuck you down the rubbish chute.'

* * *

'Sir! We've located the bike!' One of the officers whose job was to use ANPR technology to detect criminals who are on the move to avoid being caught, had spotted Carson's motor-cycle. The message quickly got back to Jack.

A convoy of police cars soon picked up its trail just as the bike got out of range of the ANPR. They tracked it to the docklands area and eventually to where it was parked outside the dilapidated warehouse. Carson had been wrong about nobody noticing or caring.

Jack and Bugsy were in the leading car and parked well out of sight in case Carson should come out and spot them. They didn't want to spook him into doing something hasty. Carefully, they crept up to the warehouse door, followed by a stealthy team of uniforms. They could hear Carson's voice inside.

'She must still be alive, guv, unless he's talking to a dead body,' whispered Bugsy.

'Now, Beatrice,' they heard him say, 'this is your chance to go to your maker, whomsoever you perceive that to be, with a clear conscience. You need to confess your sins and apologize. Say you're sorry for what you and your family did.'

Beatrice was too weak to speak so could only nod.

'Oh well, I suppose that will have to do.' He untied her from the chair, dragged her across to the trap door and pulled it open by the metal ring on the top. 'Time to go, my lady. I'd tell you to take a deep breath except I don't think it will help.'

Jack had found a gap between the broken slats and was peering through. He guessed that they needed to move and fast. He couldn't see any sign of a weapon so he shouted — 'GO!' Half a dozen coppers crashed, shouting, through the splintered door but stopped in their tracks at the sight that faced them.

Carson was hovering over the open trapdoor to the river, astride a terrified Beatrice face down, her head and shoulders already through the opening. He shouted, desperate now. 'Get back or I drop her! I mean it!'

Nobody moved, waiting for orders. Jack could hear Bugsy breathing heavily beside him, assessing whether he could jump Carson from behind and grab the old lady in one move. But it was too risky and Jack put a restraining hand on his arm.

It was Beatrice who resolved the situation. Feeling sideways along the floor, her right hand closed around one of the shards of glass from the broken windows. With her last ounce of strength, she thrust it backwards and upwards, stabbing the unsuspecting Carson in the throat. He howled with pain and surprise, lost his balance and toppled sideways still clinging on to her. That was the opportunity the officers were waiting for. They surged forwards and grabbed him, none too gently, and eased the Dowager out of his grasp. Two paramedics carried her outside on a stretcher to the waiting ambulance. There was a lot of blood but as Bugsy pointed out, blood is only scary if it's your own.

Carson was dragged away in handcuffs, struggling and screaming with rage and frustration. He had so nearly completed his mission but right at the very end, when he should have been triumphant, success had been cruelly denied by unsympathetic police.

CHAPTER TWENTY

'Bloody hell, guv. That was close.' Bugsy took a long pull at his pint. 'I thought the old girl was a goner.'

'So did I,' confessed Jack.

They were in the Richington Arms, enjoying a well-de-served drink and a pasty next to the log fire. They looked up when the door swung open and the rest of the team piled in.

'Hold up,' muttered Jack. 'It's the *Midwich Cuckoos*. I swear they've developed some kind of telepathy.'

'I blame Velma,' grinned Bugsy. 'I reckon she taught them using her mind-bending psychology hocus-pocus. On the other hand, it could just be that they're all on a WhatsApp group.'

Aled went to the bar to order drinks while the others pulled up chairs around the inglenook.

'We got him, then, sir.' Chippy was triumphant. 'It's all over the internet.'

'How could he do that to an elderly lady?' Gemma was appalled. 'I have a gran her age and it's unthinkable.'

'Do you reckon the whole story will come out now?' asked Chippy.

'I'm not sure we've heard the whole story yet.' Velma was doing her mysterious shtick.

'Do you think there's more to come in the Fitzwarren saga, then?' asked Gemma.

'Yes, I do. There's one last piece to this puzzle that we haven't yet fitted in place.'

'Well maybe we'll find the last piece when we question Carson — Barnes, that is — tomorrow,' suggested Jack.

'Hmm.' Velma chewed her lip, thoughtfully. 'Maybe — but I don't think it's Barnes who has it.'

* * *

Aled switched on the recorder and went through the protocols of requiring the people in the room to identify themselves so their voices were on record. This included the duty solicitor. They had notified Jamie Mackintosh who had declined on the basis that his father had advised him to stay well out of it.

'Right, Mr Barnes,' began Jack. 'You've been cautioned and I'm about to charge you with the murder of Lord Hugo Fitzwarren and the attempted murders of Rupert Fitzwarren and Lady Beatrice Fitzwarren. The charge regarding the death of Tracey Shuttleston has yet to be decided. Is there anything you wish to tell us?'

'Yes, plenty!' He was wearing a different 'uniform' now — still grey, but this time a tracksuit supplied by the police to prisoners in custody. 'They deserved to die — all of them. My father burned in that boat because William was drunk and out of control. There were witnesses who saw them fighting. My dad never touched alcohol, but did they believe it? — no! Because the 27th Baron of Richington couldn't possibly allow his father, a member of the proud Fitzwarren lineage, to accept the blame. When my mum tried to claim some kind of compensation, or even a small widow's pension from my dad's employment, they made her feel like a criminal and told her to go away. She died of hard work. That can't be right, can it?'

'No, but neither is taking the law into your own hands,' said Bugsy. 'There were other avenues she could have explored to get help.'

'She tried, but once the coroner had decided Dad was drunk, it was hopeless. So when I was old enough, I passed all the tests and became the Fitzwarrens' chauffeur. I applied using my mother's maiden name when the existing chauffeur retired. They had no idea who I was.'

'Was this with the intention of exacting some kind of retribution?' asked Jack.

'Not immediately, no. I was biding my time until an opportunity presented itself. But when I discovered they were planning to produce that portrait of Baron William at Beatrice's party, and everyone was saying what a distinguished and honourable gentleman he'd been, I knew the time had come to make a stand so I stuck a dagger in it, then got some red paint from one of the garages and defaced it, so everyone would know what William really was — a killer.'

'It certainly put an abrupt end to the celebrations,' recalled Jack. 'Then what?'

'I decided that the time had come to dispose of His Lordship. That last night before he vanished, I thought I'd give him a chance to own up and agree to put the record straight publicly about my father, but knowing the type of man he was, his arrogance and conceit, I had an alternative plan in place in case he refused. I drove him home from his office as usual, making sure all the CCTV cameras captured us going inside. I had already hidden a mace and the helmet on one of the shelves in the boathouse.'

'Weren't you tempted to just let it all go and get on with your life?' asked Bugsy.

Barnes straightened his shoulders. 'My heritage and the reputation of my family were just as important to me as Lord Hugo's were to him.'

'Yes, I can see that,' conceded Bugsy. 'So you lured Hugo down to the boathouse where there were no cameras.'

'That's right. After he'd been to say goodnight to Charlotte, I told him there was a problem with one of the boats and I'd like him to take a look at it. Then, when we got down there, I explained who I was and faced him with the truth.'

179

'What did he do?' Jack asked.

'He fired me. Called me a guttersnipe on the make. Told me to get out and to keep my mouth shut if I knew what was good for me. He said that nobody would believe me anyway and he was powerful enough to see to it that I never got another job. So when he turned to go, I grabbed the mace from the shelf and struck him on the back of the head.'

'Did it kill him?' asked Bugsy.

'I've no idea. But I wasn't taking any chances. I wanted him to be found drowned at Fitzwarren Hall, wearing that stupid helmet, a symbol of his weak, pathetic life and the cause of his premature, unceremonious death.'

'It certainly gave us something to think about,' acknowledged Jack.

'I wanted Beatrice to drown, too. Fire for Rupert and water for her. That's how my dad died.'

'So you targeted Rupert?'

'That was my next task. To put a stop to Rupert and Louise, before they could breed another Fitzwarren baron. I underestimated the efficiency of the emergency services who put out the fire before he was burnt to death. Obviously, I'm sorry about the woman who was with him. I had no gripe with her. I should have known, given the kind of creep he was, that he wouldn't have been sleeping with his wife. That was an oversight on my part which I regret. But I don't regret anything else. I'm just sorry you stopped me before I could finish off the old girl.'

'She's in the ICU of Kings Richington Infirmary on a heart monitoring machine,' said Bugsy, 'so you might still have succeeded.'

'Any chance of another cup of tea?' George was cool and detached, obviously unfazed by the prospect of a very long jail sentence. At a nod from Jack, the uniformed constable on the door went to fetch the tea. 'When I found out that Rupert and Charlotte weren't really Hugo's kids and the Fitzwarren line was finished, there was only Beatrice left to get rid of.'

'How did you find that out?' asked Bugsy.

'The information just fell into my lap, so to speak. Bob and Jessie found some of Hugo's papers in the priest hole and asked me to take them to Mackintosh and Mackintosh. Obviously, I picked the lock on the briefcase and looked at them before I handed them over. What a laugh! Hugo's precious kids, his hope for the future of the dynasty — they weren't his kids at all! Can you imagine how he must have felt when he found out? Someone who was so obsessed with birthright and posterity that he'd do anything to preserve it? I read his new Will cutting out his wife and her kids. The old fool was planning to marry again to try and breed another heir. Well, it was obviously my duty as a citizen and member of the Kings Richington community to make sure the information got out, so I leaked it to the *Echo*.'

That would explain, thought Jack, *how Cynthia Garwood's Ladies Luncheon Club got wind of the story that Lord Hugo was a 'jaffa'. News certainly spread fast in this community.* 'One last question before I charge you, Mr Barnes. Why did you start the earlier fires out at Fitzwarren Farm?'

George looked puzzled. 'What fires?'

'The one where Lord Hugo was trapped in the barn and then when his quad bike caught fire.'

'I don't know what you mean. The only fire I started was at the Fitz Gallery.'

'Chummy had no reason to lie,' observed Bugsy afterwards. 'He'd already coughed to everything else.'

'Now that we've solved the Fitzwarren murder to everybody's satisfaction, including a grudging Garwood, I think, tomorrow, we should take a trip out to Fitzwarren Farm and have a chat with Adam Baker.'

* * *

Next morning saw Jack and Bugsy driving deep into the heart of the Cotswolds, where each village quickly blended into the next. *This part of the country is certainly no stranger to a good pub,* thought Bugsy as they passed several that he reckoned would serve a good pint. But they were headed for The Dog and Rabbit at Benfield-under-Wychwood. Clad in ivy and once a 17th-century tavern, it was very popular with the locals, particularly at lunchtimes. According to what one of the farm workers had told the two police officers when they arrived at Fitzwarren Farm, this was where they would find Adam, Danielle and Charlotte. It was just a stone's throw from the farm and they had gone there for a quick lunch and a family conference.

Charlie recognized the detectives as soon as they pushed open the pub door. 'Inspector Dawes and Sergeant Malone. You caught the man who killed my Pa. Thank you.'

Adam pulled two more chairs across to the table and they sat down. 'Is it true what everyone's saying, Inspector? It was that young chauffeur? I can't believe it. He'd driven Lord Hugo to the farm loads of times and I would never have suspected him of anything violent. Such a polite chap and so interested in the farm and the livestock. We even invited him in and gave him lunch, didn't we, Charlie?'

'That's what makes our job so difficult, Mr Baker. The murderer is rarely who you think it is.' Jack sipped the cup of tea that Bugsy had so thoughtfully ordered him because he was driving, while noticing that Bugsy, himself, was sampling a pint of the local ale and a cheese roll, with every sign of enjoyment.

'What brings you all the way out here to the countryside, officers?' asked Charlie. 'I'm sure it wasn't just to tell me that you'd arrested George.'

'No, miss,' replied Bugsy, wondering if he should have ordered a roll for Jack. 'There are just a few loose ends we need to tie up.'

'It's to do with the fires here when the late Lord Hugo was trapped in a burning barn and his quad bike burst into flames.' Jack watched for any reaction.

'I guess that was down to George as well. But Dani was on the ball though, Inspector Dawes,' Adam said. 'She was in there straight away with a fire extinguisher both times, weren't you, love?' He looked at her proudly.

'Yes, Dad.' She pushed her Ploughman's Lunch around the plate without much enthusiasm until finally, a pickled onion rolled off and onto the floor.

'The thing is,' began Jack, 'when we interviewed Barnes, he denied having anything to do with it.'

'And did you believe him?' asked Charlie.

'Yes, miss, we did,' confirmed Bugsy. 'Because he admitted to all the other crimes he'd committed. He had no reason not to ask for those fires to be taken into account, too.'

'Is it possible that it might have been one of your farm workers with some kind of grudge?' asked Jack. 'Perhaps we should ask the local police to send in a team to question your workers just in case . . .'

'No!' said Dani, suddenly. 'You don't need to do that. It was me. I started the fires. But I was always waiting nearby with an extinguisher. I never intended for him to be hurt.'

Adam and Charlie looked at her in surprise. 'Dani, whatever for?' asked Adam. 'Why would you do such a dangerous thing? Fire on a farm is a massive risk with so much that can catch alight. You must know that.'

'Yes, Dad, and I'm sorry. I just wanted to teach him a lesson in humility. I was so angry at the way he spoke to Charlie when she said she wanted to come and live here with me. All that pompous rubbish about how such a relationship would damage the fine reputation of the Fitzwarrens built up over a thousand years.'

'Especially now we know that I'm not even a Fitzwarren,' agreed Charlie. She put an arm around Dani who was crying quietly into her napkin. 'Pa was always good to me, even when I kept getting chucked out of school, but I have to wonder if he would have been the same if he'd known I wasn't his daughter.'

'So, Inspector, what will you do now?' asked Adam. 'Are you going to charge my daughter? She has confessed and said

183

she's sorry. She knows it was foolish but she never intended for any real harm to come to Lord Hugo.'

'Well, starting a fire deliberately knowing someone might be at risk is certainly a crime, Mr Baker. But as a police officer, my view has always been — and I've said it on several occasions — that sometimes, in the interests of compassion, it's necessary to jam a stick in the wheels of justice. Please don't do it again, Dani.'

'No, I won't. I promise. Thank you.'

'Where do you go from here, Mr Baker?' asked Bugsy. 'I understand Lord Hugo had transferred the deeds of the farm to Charlie some time ago.'

'We were just discussing that when you came in, Sergeant. Obviously, without ongoing support from the Fitzwarren estate, we have to find an alternative income stream. We've decided to open up as a petting farm. I've bought a few alpacas and some small animals, rabbits and guinea pigs, and together with the rest of our rare breeds, we should be able to keep the farm going.'

'We're looking forward to it, Inspector,' said Charlie. 'It's a challenge but if we work hard and our volunteers stay with us, I'm sure it will be a success.'

'I wish you the very best of luck.' Jack and Bugsy got up to leave and Charlie gave each of them a hug.

'We're changing the name,' Charlie told them. 'It isn't Fitzwarren Farm any more. It's going to be called Farmyard Friends.'

CHAPTER TWENTY-ONE

Sir Leonard had wanted Beatrice transferred to the private hospital where he had performed many life-saving heart operations, but he could see that she was too fragile to be moved just yet. He sat at her bedside, day and night, for over a week until she started to show improvement.

After what she had been through, Jack reckoned it was a minor miracle that Dowager Beatrice was still alive. All the same, he had to visit her to obtain her statement before George Barnes' trial. Hers was important evidence and it wasn't something he wanted to delegate. He took Velma with him to record the statement. A witness was required in an important case like this. Added to which, he didn't want any accusations of police 'verbals' — alleged words that might implicate her in something but that she didn't actually say.

Sir Leonard wasn't best pleased to see him. 'Oh really, Inspector, is this absolutely necessary? You have the man's confession. Isn't that enough?'

'I'm sorry, Sir Leonard, but we really do need Lady Beatrice's account.'

'It's all right, Monty. I can do this. Now that I know who George Carson really is, the police need to set the record straight. I can see that.' She turned to Jack. 'He really was going to kill me, wasn't he?'

'Oh yes. I think he would have, if we hadn't intervened when we did. He was seeking some kind of retribution for the alleged treatment of his father by you and Lord Hugo. He believed you influenced the coroner to blame Sid Barnes for the boat accident that killed your late husband, in order to preserve your public image.' *And more to the point*, thought Jack, *to avoid any financial responsibility.*

Beatrice seemed to be considering her position before continuing. 'George was quite right — we did lie. In order for you to understand, I need to take you back many years to when William and I were married. We were very young and William was consumed with the need to continue the ancient line of the Fitzwarren barons. Indeed, it was his family rather than William who selected me for the dubious privilege of becoming the mother of the next baron. I came from a fecund family and I knew how to behave so as not to bring any kind of dishonour on their esteemed name.' She paused and reached for a glass of water.

'Are you sure you're happy to continue, my lady?' Jack didn't want accusations of police insensitivity. He glanced across at Velma who was recording the interview on her phone.

'Yes, I'm fine. Please let me explain why I did what I did. We had been married for two years and every month when I continued to menstruate, I had to report to William and his family that I still had not conceived. It was feudal and humiliating. He was a big, powerful man with anger issues and he would fly into a rage every time, calling me worthless and pathetic. He was also drinking far too much, believing that kind of behaviour was acceptable for someone of his status in the peerage. Anyway, suffice it to say I found comfort and solace in the arms of Sidney Barnes, the Fitzwarrens' chauffeur. He was very young too and we made love in the back of the Rolls Royce, late at night while William was sleeping off another bout of drinking. Two months later I was pregnant and seven months after that, Hugo was born.'

'Did Hugo know he wasn't a legitimate heir?' asked Jack, wondering how much more complicated this saga could get.

'No, he didn't, and I would never have told him. He would have been devastated. His whole life was predicated upon being born into a long and illustrious line of barons. Had he known he was just a chauffeur's son, it would have destroyed him.'

'What about Sid Barnes?' asked Sir Leonard. 'Did he know?'

'He must have done but he said nothing to the family. He wanted me to leave William and marry him but obviously I couldn't.'

'Why not?' Sir Leonard was looking increasingly shocked by what he was hearing. 'If you loved him and he loved you, what else mattered?'

'Being a baroness and everything that went with it mattered a great deal. And now that I'd given birth to a son, William left me alone. Poor Sidney waited years for me until he finally gave up and married Eileen. She was one of the household, a parlour maid, I think. And of course, she eventually gave birth to George Barnes. That's why he is so much younger than Hugo.'

'Do you know what happened on the motorboat?' asked Jack.

'That's when everything went wrong. William had been comparing himself to Hugo. William was over six feet tall and heavily built, with a ruddy complexion and a shock of iron-grey hair. Hugo, as you know, was short with thin mousy hair, a pasty complexion and a big nose. He was, in fact, the image of Sidney, his father, and eventually, during one of his drinking binges, William became suspicious. He challenged me — grabbed me by the throat and shook me like a rag doll until I thought he was going to strangle me. I had to tell him the truth. It was while he was in this blind drunken rage that he demanded Sidney took him out in the boat. I don't know what his intentions were. Maybe he had some half-baked idea that he would knock Sid out and throw him over the side to drown. William was uncontrolled and irrational when he was drunk. But the witnesses were quite right when they said the two men were fighting when they lost control and hit the bridge. The rest you know.' She sank back against the pillows, exhausted.

That's it! thought Velma, triumphantly. *The last piece of the puzzle. The real reason for the crash that only Beatrice knew. And if the coroner had been told, the verdict of the inquest might have been completely different. Sid Barnes may not have been accused posthumously of causing death by careless driving while under the influence of drink and George Barnes's mother might have been entitled to some compensation.*

Jack didn't quite know what to say. The fallout from these revelations was wide-ranging. He guessed that George Barnes would eventually have to be told that he had murdered his half-brother, but he didn't think that was a police job. Probably more the responsibility of whoever was appointed to assess his mental state before he was convicted and sentenced.

'Monty, dear, I've changed my mind.' Beatrice reached for his hand. 'I will come and live with you, when I get out of this nasty, cheap little hospital. Your house is adequate and I'm sure I'll get used to the lack of space.'

Sir Leonard shook her off. 'I've changed my mind, too, Beatrice. You forget, I was in the solicitor's office that day when you called Helena's children 'bastard brats'. You slapped her and called her a whore, all the time knowing that you'd done exactly the same thing to produce an heir as she had. I can't believe you could be such a spiteful hypocrite and I certainly don't want you to live with me.'

Beatrice burst into tears. 'But Monty, where will I go? What shall I do for money?'

He stood up. 'That's really not my problem. There's a perfectly good, council-run, old people's home less than a mile away. I suggest you apply to live there and hope they have a vacancy.' He strode out of the room with scarcely a backward glance.

Outside in the police car, Jack was still trying to process what he'd heard. 'Did you get all that, Velma?'

'Yes, sir. All of it.'

'You were right. There was a last piece missing from the puzzle.'

'Yes, sir.'

He shook his head. 'What a way to live. You couldn't make it up. Aren't you glad you're not one of the aristocracy with a fancy title and absolutely no moral compass whatsoever?'

'Yes, sir.'

* * *

'My goodness, Jack, no wonder you look strained.' Corrie could tell from his furrowed brow and weary manner that he'd had a harder than usual day and after he'd recounted Beatrice's confession, she understood why. She poured him a beer while the dinner cooked and he sank down into an armchair.

'I have to admit, I found it pretty stressful. All the lies, deceit and betrayal for years and years, just to maintain some kind of barmy pretence at being more entitled than everyone else. I'd find it exhausting.'

'So would I, darling. But in some quarters, that kind of thing still opens doors. You only had to look at the turnout at Lady Beatrice's birthday party. You're not telling me that all those people got scrubbed up and turned out just to wish an old lady happy birthday. It carries a kind of kudos to be able to say you were invited and you get to rub shoulders with a lot of influential people.'

'Well, I don't know about you but it makes me feel kind of grubby to have been there at all. Paying some kind of cheap homage to a family who have to depend on their phoney birth-right to earn respect.'

'OK, Che Guevara. Enough of this Marxist talk. Come and have your supper.'

'What is it?'

'Steak and kidney pudding followed by jam roly-poly and custard. I can hear your arteries protesting already.'

He grinned. 'Yes, but my stomach is cheering.'

* * *

The whole Fitzwarren narrative had shaken up everyone who knew the family and a good deal of folk who didn't, thanks to the editor of the *Echo*. Despite warnings from the Press Office that a court case was pending and some details were *sub judice* so could not be discussed, it was too good an opportunity to be missed. He had run a centre-page spread, documenting every detail, from the early days of Lord William and Lady Beatrice to the present day and the end of the lineage, including the impending insolvency and the takeover of Fitzwarren Hall by Sheikh bin Ali. The headline was *The Fall of the House of Fitzwarren*.

The gossip in the London gentlemen's club was almost enough to rival the last meeting of Cynthia Garwood's Ladies Luncheon Club, albeit slightly below it in the decibel range. Angus Mackintosh was finding it difficult to find a seat until Commander Sir Barnaby made room for him on the giant leather Chesterfield sofa.

'Bit of a rum do, the Fitzwarren business, Scotty. I suppose you knew all about it, being the family lawyer?' He drained his glass and motioned to the steward for two more.

'Actually, Commander, things have come to light that even we didn't know about. The Fitzwarrens certainly knew how to play their cards close to their chest.'

Barnaby looked around, then put his mouth close to Scotty's ear. 'Bloody close thing for the old lady. It was touch and go at one point, I don't mind telling you. If my chaps hadn't been on the ball, she'd be floating down the Thames like an empty burger box.'

'Really?' They paused while the steward brought the drinks. 'Jamie's handling the paperwork for the CPS,' said Angus. 'He reckons George Barnes is on a hiding to nothing unless the trick cyclists can scrape together something with lots of capital letters that they believe he's suffering from. I expect they'll dredge up undiagnosed problems from his childhood. That's what usually happens.'

'Is it right the estate is insolvent?' asked Barnaby.

'Aye, it is. They don't have a pot to pish in,' declared Scotty.

'What will happen to Fitzwarren Hall, then?' The Commander had always regarded it as one of the last local strongholds of British history.

'It's been sold to Sheikh bin Ali . . . something or other, an oil magnate from Abu Dhabi. He's keeping it exactly as it is and all the staff as well. Going to use it as a conference centre where his business delegates can stay when they come over. All that medieval paraphernalia is very popular, apparently.'

'I suppose someone has told him that most of the artefacts are fakes?' suggested Barnaby.

'I don't think it matters, old man.'

* * *

The MIT incident room had a decided atmosphere of anticlimax. It had been a long, drawn-out investigation with many twists and turns before culminating in what was widely regarded as a successful outcome. Aled had cleaned the whiteboard which was now pristine, awaiting the next onslaught of photos and scribbled snippets of information that accompanied a murder enquiry.

'Well, folks, I guess we should all leave early, while we've got the chance,' announced Jack.

Bugsy was unusually thoughtful. 'It makes you wonder, though, doesn't it?'

'Wonder what, Sarge?' asked Aled, pulling on his jacket.

'All that stuff about heritage and rightful heirs to a title. I mean, when you think how long all those knights and barons were away from home fighting battles abroad and their wives were left at home to amuse themselves, how could any of them be absolutely sure that their sons were really their sons?'

'So you reckon all those families who claim they can trace their ancestry back a thousand years in an unbroken line are being ingenuous, Sarge?' said Chippy.

'Yeah, I do, and it's just as well they believed what they were told. You saw what happened when Baron William and Baron Hugo became suspicious. It didn't end well.'

'*A man hears what he wants to hear and disregards the rest,*' quoted Velma.

'Did Nietzsche say that?' asked Aled.

'No, Paul Simon actually, but the theory is sound.'

'Enough philosophy,' decided Jack. 'Everyone down the pub. The first round's on me.'

They were piling out of the door, chatting amongst themselves, when the phone rang. Bugsy being the last one out, answered it. He shouted across to them as they were leaving. 'Hold up, folks! They've found a body in Richington Forest . . .'

EPILOGUE

In any conflict, whether medieval or modern, there are winners and losers. The catastrophic sequence of events that brought about the downfall of the Fitzwarren family had resulted mostly in losers.

* * *

Lord Hugo Fitzwarren, 27th Baron of Richington (deceased)

Lord Hugo paid for his life-long hubris when he discovered he had been duped by his wife and that he was not the father of a legitimate heir to the Fitzwarren title. His exaggerated pride and embellished view of his ancestry ended abruptly when he was killed in a 'Cain and Abel' type murder by his half-brother. Had he lived long enough, Hugo might have discovered that he had been similarly duped by his mother and that he was, in fact, the son of a chauffeur and not a baron. It might have been enough to change his attitude to those people he regarded as inferior. But then again, it might not.

* * *

Lady Beatrice Fitzwarren, Dowager Baroness of Richington

With her son dead and Sir Leonard Montgomery, her gentle-man friend of many years, now alienated, Beatrice found herself homeless, penniless and friendless. With no staff to wait on her, no Dower House to live in, and no money to support a privi-leged lifestyle, she ended up in a council-funded care home for the elderly. The staff called her Beattie, despite her protestations that the correct form of address was 'my lady'. She treated the other residents with equal contempt and during one heated altercation over the ownership of a cashmere cardigan, she suc-cumbed to a massive and final heart attack. Since no one came forward to claim responsibility, she was given a Public Health Funeral paid for by Kings Richington Council.

* * *

The Honourable Rupert Fitzwarren

Shocked at finding himself without any of the advantages that had come with his previous situation, Rupert discovered that for the first time in his life, he needed to earn a living. When the bal-loon went up at the reading of the Will and he found out he was the son of a gigolo posing as a ski instructor, he gave it some seri-ous thought. After some research, he offered his services to an upmarket escort agency in Mayfair. With his mouth-watering good looks, sartorial good taste and blue-blooded background, they snapped him up immediately. He rapidly became the most in demand and highest paid operative on their books. It was only later, after a mandatory health check, that they discovered his 'handicap' and the lawsuits started coming in.

* * *

Lady Helena Fitzwarren

When Helena was finally forced to accept that Dickie Napier-Smythe had absconded with all the loot and wasn't coming back for her, she returned to modelling, the only work she knew. Only this time, her splendidly preserved figure was irrelevant. She was featuring in advertisements for cleaning materials and most of the shots were of her hands, usually wearing rubber gloves, and scrubbing ovens. Both children had abandoned her with scarcely a backward glance. Instead of champagne, she now had to make do with cheap Prosecco. Her only consolation was knowing that Beatrice, the evil old cow, had been put in a home, and knowing how much she would be hating it.

* * *

George Barnes (Carson)

Despite representation from defence counsel that his actions were the consequence of a traumatic childhood and he was suffering from a number of personality disorders, the judge was having none of it. George was given a life sentence with a recommendation that he serve at least twenty-five years before any parole could be considered. He accepted his sentence with calm equanimity. His only regret, he said, was that he had been unable to finish his quest by disposing of the Dowager Beatrice Fitzwarren, before he was arrested. When he was told that she had once been his father's mistress, it didn't appear to make any difference, nor did the realization that he had, in fact, murdered his half-brother. As far as George was concerned, Beatrice had colluded with Lord Hugo in the wicked lies about his father and the cruel rejection of his mother. For that, they both deserved to die.

* * *

Dickie Napier-Smythe

The National Crime Agency works tirelessly to track the complex movement of funds across the international banking system through shell companies and in multiple jurisdictions.

It was thus that a particularly clever young woman in their employ spotted a disconnect in money moving from a UK finance company, Fitzwarren & Napier-Smythe Asset Management, to various banks in the Caymans. She decided to investigate and the result would have impressed even a life-long technical expert like Clive, and his digital forensics team. It culminated in the identification of Dickie Napier-Smythe and his subsequent extradition back to the UK. Much of the money was recovered and returned to its rightful owners. His lengthy prison sentence meant he would be unavailable for any kind of financial transactions for some time to come and it demonstrated what happens if you try to outrun the mounting consequences of your dubious deeds.

* * *

The only winners, if they could be called that, to survive the Fitzwarren debacle and go on to lead relatively happy lives, were sparse. But in the main, they were those individuals who had managed to avoid the lies and deceit of an anachronistic and self-serving family.

* * *

The Honourable Charlotte (Charlie) Fitzwarren

The petting farm in the Cotswolds, 'Farmyard Friends', took off immediately. The animals were carefully tended, healthy and content. Visitors, including eager children, were invited to bottle-feed the lambs, groom the ponies, feed the chickens, ducks and geese and pet the small animals. It developed into a very lucrative enterprise and happy in her partnership with Dani, Charlie blossomed. She never forgot her Pa but the memories of each of her parents and their consequences became less vivid as time went on.

* * *

Louise Fraser (Fitzwarren)

Back in Scotland, surrounded by friends and relatives, Louise returned to the job she'd loved before her ill-fated marriage to Rupert. She had already gained the necessary qualifications in childcare so with financial help from her parents, she opened a nursery. If she could never have babies of her own, she decided, she would care for other people's. And so it was that 'Lulu's Ladybirds' was created and flourished. She was happy for the first time in years.

* * *

Bob and Jessie Beach

True to his word, the Sheikh who bought Fitzwarren Hall retained all the staff — Bob and Jessie, Ted Greenslade and his team of gardeners, even Winnie the Pinny to deal with the laundry. When Sheikh bin Ali asked, politely, why there was no one to drive the cars, he was told, equally politely, that the chauffeur had to leave in something of a hurry.

THE END

THE JOFFE BOOKS STORY

We began in 2014 when Jasper agreed to publish his mum's much-rejected romance novel and it became a bestseller.

Since then we've grown into the largest independent publisher in the UK. We're extremely proud to publish some of the very best writers in the world, including Joy Ellis, Faith Martin, Caro Ramsay, Helen Forrester, Simon Brett and Robert Goddard. Everyone at Joffe Books loves reading and we never forget that it all begins with the magic of an author telling a story.

We are proud to publish talented first-time authors, as well as established writers whose books we love introducing to a new generation of readers.

We won Trade Publisher of the Year at the Independent Publishing Awards in 2023 and Best Publisher Award in 2024 at the People's Book Prize. We have been shortlisted for Independent Publisher of the Year at the British Book Awards for the last five years, and were shortlisted for the Diversity and Inclusivity Award at the 2022 Independent Publishing Awards. In 2023 we were shortlisted for Publisher of the Year at the RNA Industry Awards, and in 2024 we were shortlisted at the CWA Daggers for the Best Crime and Mystery Publisher.

We built this company with your help, and we love to hear from you, so please email us about absolutely anything bookish at feedback@joffebooks.com.

If you want to receive free books every Friday and hear about all our new releases, join our mailing list here: www.joffe-books.com/freebooks.

And when you tell your friends about us, just remember: it's pronounced Joffe as in coffee or toffee!

www.ingramcontent.com/pod-product-compliance
Ingram Content Group UK Ltd.
Pitfield, Milton Keynes, MK11 3LW, UK
UKHW030629240225
4724UKWH00040B/256

9 781805 730057